30 Minutes in Memphis

A Beatles Story

PAUL FERRANTE

Dedication

To Beatles fans everywhere
Who continue to pass the torch
and
To John, Paul, George and Ringo
Thanks for everything you've given me.

Acknowledgments

As a Beatlephile who has consumed virtually everything on the Fab Four, there are four works that stood out for me in the research for this project: *The Beatles* by Bob Spitz (2006), *Beatles '66: The Revolutionary Year* by Steve Turner (2016), and the documentaries *The Beatles Anthology* (1996) and Ron Howard's *The Beatles: 8 Days a Week—The Touring Years* (2016). I'm also appreciative for the personal direction given by Julia Baird, John Lennon's sister, in the cover design and title reboot.

During the writing of this book I immersed myself in my Beatles records at home and the wonderful Beatles Sirius XM radio station in my car. To this day the scope of their music from 1962-1970 is mind-boggling to me. And though works of a biographical nature have cast these four remarkable people in a sometimes-unflattering light, both as a unit and individually, in the end it's about the music, and a moment in time that will never be recaptured.

For the sake of historical accuracy, this paperback writer has tried not to change any dates or times of the events herein, but the advanced Beatles aficionado might detect a minor tweak here or there to facilitate plot flow. Hopefully, this will not detract from your enjoyment of the story. Just relax and float downstream.

Prologue
August 19, 2016

The woman emerged from her silver Nissan SUV onto the hot macadam surface of a barren parking lot, the car's frigid air-conditioning a stark contrast to the steamy, high 80s climate. She removed the light jacket she'd worn on the long drive to get here and threw it back onto the driver's seat before using the remote to lock up. Then she moved towards the only other car in the lot, a black BMW sedan, some twenty feet away.

A man stood in front of the Beemer, his back to her. She guessed his height at about six-one, with the familiar bony shoulders that caused one to imagine he'd neglected to remove the clothes hanger from his black golf shirt before putting it on. Playfully, she sneaked up on him, but a tap on the shoulder failed to elicit a cry of surprise. Instead, he turned to her and they embraced, the top of her head well below his chin. "I'm glad you came," he murmured into her thick brown hair. The two held each other tightly for a few more seconds, then stood at arm's length, holding hands.

"You look the same," she said, shaking her head in wondrous approval.

"No, I don't," he replied wryly, "but I thank you for making my day."

"I mean it, seriously!" she countered, her accent breaking through to where "I" sounded like "Ah." "Okay, so there's some gray in there, but you've still got that curly mop. But where are your glasses?"

"I switched to contacts long ago, which allow me to see that you, my dear, are as stunning as ever." He perused her with a broad grin. "I'll bet you still play a mean game of tennis. You've cut your hair, though."

"Yeah, that happened around 1990. Figured I was getting too old for the *mod* look. And you don't want to know how gray it'd be without my monthly coloring." She squinted through the hazy sunlight. "Tell you what, though. That ol' thing over there still looks the same." She nodded towards a large object in the distance.

"It's a relic, like us," he joked.

"Speak for y'self."

They shared a laugh and peered across the cracked parking lot at a domed structure resembling a whitewashed spaceship resting on its concrete launchpad—or maybe a half-cooked container of Jiffy Pop.

"I can't believe they haven't torn it down yet," she marveled. "What're they waiting on? It's been vacant for like ten years, I'm told."

"There are all kinds of theories and proposals," he explained. "Some groups want to demolish it for a fairgrounds or recreation complex; some want to restore it. The city government's been wrestling with the problem for years, and they're not getting anywhere. There's another hearing later this month."

She nodded, a trickle of sweat tracking its way down the side of her face. He deftly flicked it aside.

"Thanks," she said, "I almost forgot how god-awful the weather is here in August."

"Betcha it's cooler in there," he said, inclining his head towards the building.

"But it's locked up tight, isn't it?"

He smiled impishly. "Not quite," he gently corrected. "I know a way in."

"Should we?"

"How could we *not*?"

"But won't you, you know, get in some kind of trouble? A guy in your position?"

"Nah," he said with a chuckle. "I've got friends in high places, remember."

"Okay, then," she said conspiratorially. "Let's do it. Lead the way."

Minutes later, after crossing the vast parking lot and skirting the perimeter of the building, the man comically cast furtive glances in both directions, then eased open a service entrance door with a busted lock. "Still want to do it?" he whispered teasingly.

"Why not?" she replied, stepping through the portal into the gloomy darkness of the deserted Mid-South Coliseum. "It's only been fifty years."

Chapter One
May, 1966

"Marnie Culpeper, you get your behind down here right now and eat your breakfast before you're late to school!" Tillie's voice bounced off the stairwell walls and reverberated in the bedroom where the fifteen-year-old lay, her long tresses a swirl enveloping her head and blotting out the sun streaming through her window. It never failed; her housekeeper blurted the same warning every single day of the school year. Thank God today was her last one—as a junior high schooler, anyway.

Yawning loudly, Marnie blindly reached out and brought her hand down on a button switch mounted to the top of her nightstand. The button activated a contraption that would have made Rube Goldberg envious; a series of levers and pulleys snaked up the wall behind the nightstand and over to a nearby table where her record player lay, its fliptop open and a shiny vinyl LP awaiting.

A final pulley gently lowered the phonograph needle onto the activated turntable, and the Lennon-McCartney composition "I'll Cry Instead," the first track of the *Something New* album of 1964—the Beatles' fifth release in the States—sprang to life. The record had been selected the night before and carefully slipped from its sheathing that featured a color photograph of the group performing during its historic Ed Sullivan appearance. Marnie had gently set it in place before she took her nightly shower, dried her hair, and brushed it 100 times exactly to bring out the luster, a technique she'd read about in *Seventeen* magazine. Whereas many of her female schoolmates were doing the bouffant thing—along with some holdover beehives, mostly from the "country" crowd—Marnie had gone to the much more "mod" center part favored by British girls, her locks falling halfway down her back. Of course, this often presented a problem, like right now, as it was cocooned around her head.

She sat up and cleared the hair from her face, yawned again, and padded off to the upstairs bathroom where she washed up, sprayed on some deodorant, and brushed her teeth (why, she didn't know; she was going to eat breakfast anyway). Then it was time to slip into her preferred school attire that she sported at Hillcrest Junior High School—namely, a Beatles tee shirt and jeans. Most of the time, though, she did put on a skirt or dress like the other girls, and that was just to get the school administrators, and Tillie, off her back for a while. Besides, she knew the housekeeper was just acting upon orders from The Sarge.

After pulling on her Converse Chuck Taylors, Marnie sat at her overflowing makeup table and ran a brush through her hair. She had an oval face, with a slightly upturned nose and a spray of freckles across her cheeks that made her look younger, though she'd heard the boys at school had classified her as "cute." On this day, besides her sleepy brown eyes staring back at her, the mirror was edged with magazine photos of the four people who were at the epicenter of her life, boys named John, Paul, George and Ringo. In fact, there was scarcely a space on her bedroom walls that *wasn't* occupied by the lads from Liverpool. The only reason they weren't on the ceiling as well was because the scotch tape wouldn't hold in the Memphis humidity.

She spritzed on some Yardley perfume (the brand of choice with British girls), rose from the chair as the last strains of "Any Time at All" drifted across the room, and deftly lifted the needle from the LP before switching off the phonograph (Myles hadn't figured out a way to rig that up yet) and returning the record to its sleeve. Then it was down the stairs in a rush to where Tillie was pouring some Rice Krispies into her official Beatles Fan Club cereal bowl.

"Seriously, Miss Marnie," she chided, "is it so important for you to eat out of a bowl with those bugs on it?" She always called them "those bugs" to get a rise out of her, but it was hard to get mad at Tillie. She was a holdover from Marnie's mom, who had run off with a used car salesman in December of '63, just before the Christmas holiday, no less. Marnie and her dad had been in a bad enough funk over the death of President Kennedy, and although the girl had kind of seen it coming, her mom's desertion had been a jolt nonetheless, a heartless betrayal that had deeply wounded her father and left her embittered.

It was hard to tell how old Tillie was. Her short Afro-bouffant was shot through with gray, but she had a young face of smooth, milk chocolate skin. In her pink housekeeper outfit, she wasn't exactly curvy, more along the lines of "solidly built." Marnie had more than once seen Tillie heft bulging bags of groceries one-handed that she could barely lift with both. And the housekeeper's family situation was kind of mysterious. All Marnie knew about Tillie was that she lived in one of the poorer Negro neighborhoods in town, had a son who was planning to enter the Marine Corps, and twin girls who attended a different school from hers. Tillie's husband was a construction laborer who sometimes went long stretches without work, so this job was important to her, and she was diligent about it if nothing else. And though it was tough for Marnie's dad to retain her services on a policeman's salary, he recognized the woman's value as a stabilizing female influence in his daughter's life. It was Tillie who had guided her through some early boy crushes ("Don't pay him no nevermind, my dear, he ain't deserving of you."), the purchase of her first bra ("Ain't much for it to hold in place now, but if you take after your momma, there will be soon enough."), and her first period ("It's just the Lord's way of reminding you that you're becoming a woman, and that your body is a temple."). Other things, such as shaving her legs and the application of makeup, had been learned through trial and error, with an assist from the columnists of *Seventeen* magazine.

Of course, Tillie's most invaluable role was as a buffer between the flighty teenaged girl and her father. Indeed, there weren't many women who could deal with Sgt. Roy Culpeper without shrinking back or— like Marnie's mom—running off. But Tillie could be just as ornery when she had to, and The Sarge respected that.

"Tillie, you say the same thing every time you make my cereal," Marnie moaned as she added milk and awaited the famous snap-crackle-pop of the Krispies. "When are you going to accept that the Beatles are here to stay?"

"When the Lord shakes me awake some night and tells me, 'Tillie dear, don't be hard on those bugs, they're just British boys that don't know how silly they look, or how sinful their music is.'"

"Aw, c'mon," Marnie retorted while sipping some fresh squeezed orange juice, "you know as well as I do that their heroes are Negro singers."

"Oh, really? Such as who?"

"Well, Chuck Berry, for one."

"The one been in trouble with the law?"

"And Fats Domino."

"Boy who cain't even control his appetite, and flashes all that gaudy jewelry?"

"How about Little Richard?"

At the mention of this name the housekeeper just rolled her eyes and said, "Don't even get me started on *that* one!"

Marnie couldn't help but laugh. "Okay, okay," she relented, "but they also look up to Elvis. Now c'mon, Tillie, you can't say you don't like Memphis's number one son."

"'Cept he's really from Mississippi. White boy who tries to sing like a colored man, shakin' his hips and whatnot? Hm-mm-mm." She paused for a moment, then softened a bit. "Although he does love his mama, and that's a fact. And when he sets his mind to singing gospel, he's got a right pretty voice. Actually, he's kinda pretty himself, truth be told." She actually arched an eyebrow, which sent Marnie into hysterics.

"But let me point out," Tillie added sternly, catching herself, "he don't look like some girl with a cereal bowl haircut. That boy's served Uncle Sam just like my son's going to, and with a proper haircut, no less!"

Marnie tipped the bowl to her lips and slurped the last of the sweet milk—a habit Tillie detested—and said, "You win, you win. But I still love the lads."

It was while Marnie was at her lowest ebb that she'd first heard "I Want to Hold Your Hand" on WHBQ, the first local radio station to play Elvis's songs a decade earlier. It had been a school morning such as this one, and she was at the breakfast table. For some reason, Tillie had her transistor radio playing on the kitchen counter, when suddenly the woman exclaimed, "What in the *world*?" Strange sounds were emanating from that little box.

Marnie had lifted her head from whatever she was eating. "Turn it up!" she'd said excitedly. What she heard was so new, so fresh and vibrant and *positive*, that she stopped chewing and sat, enraptured, until the conclusion of the song and awaited the motormouthed deejay's comments:

"And those are the Beatles, spelled with an A, the new pop combo who are stirring things up in the British Isles and finding their way onto the charts here in the US of A. We've been getting numerous requests to play their songs, and there's no better place to hear your fabulous faves than Boss Radio WHBQ, so here's another one from the lads from Liverpool called 'All My Loving'!"

She was inextricably hooked. And while it was true that Marnie Culpepper had religiously read *Tiger Beat* and other teen magazines for info on such early 60s teen idols as Fabian and Frankie Avalon and had enjoyed the tunes of vocal groups like the Four Seasons, Beach Boys, and even some Motown acts like the Supremes and Temptations, this was something utterly different. Something that reached into her chest and flooded her heart. *Something to hold onto.*

These guys were cute, with their matching haircuts, Edwardian suits and Beatle boots. But they were also witty and personable, not to mention that they could sing up a storm—in short, everything the twelve-year-old Marnie would want in a boy. So, when it was announced that the Beatles would be coming to the US for a tour commencing with an appearance on the *Ed Sullivan Show* on February 9, 1964, Marnie and her dad tuned in on their Magnavox black and white TV, as did much of America, to see what all the fuss was about.

Predictably, their reactions ran along generational lines. Roy Culpeper, Korean War combat veteran and sergeant in the Memphis PD, a crewcut, spit-and-polish, no nonsense guy whose taste ran to Hank Williams and Buck Owens, was understandably appalled. "I'm missing *Bonanza* for *this*?" he'd moaned. "Are those guys or gals?"

"Oh, Daddy, stop," she'd replied in her most disarming little-girl voice. "They have suits and ties on. I think they're cute."

"Kittens are cute. Boys are supposed to be handsome... and manly."

"I think *you're* cute, Daddy," she'd offered, which made him smile and shake his cinderblock-shaped head.

"Well, at least they can carry a tune," he'd conceded grudgingly. "Ah, well, no harm done, darlin'. They're just a passing fad, you'll see."

But he was wrong, at least where his daughter was concerned. Because while the Beatles quickly became popular at Marnie's school (prompting quickly instituted rules outlawing hairstyles on boys that covered their ears or fell below the tops of their shirt collars) Marnie took it to another level, becoming totally immersed in everything Beatle. She saved enough from her meager allowance to buy every teen magazine or piece of paraphernalia that had a Beatles likeness on it. Record albums and 45s were requested as special birthday or Christmas gifts. And her viewings of *A Hard Day's Night* and *Help!* at the local movie house were so numerous for Marnie (most of the time accompanied by her best friend, Charlotte Perkins, whose passion for the boys was not nearly as fervent) that she had pretty much memorized the dialogue from both films and quoted from them frequently, her Southern drawl mixing awkwardly with the Fabs' Liverpudlian lilt.

Of course, when her obsession with the group did not wane, everyone who was associated with Marnie, including her father, teachers and classmates, began to wonder if this was all a giant compensation for the loss of her mother, an escape from reality of sorts. The only person who seemed to "get it" was her friend Myles Goldfarb, architect of her record player apparatus. Like her, Myles, one of the first boys to be reprimanded when his curly dark hair began to hang too low for the junior high administration's taste, was considered a bit odd, both because he was virtually the only Jew in their class—a New York transplant, no less—and because he seemingly went out of his way to tweak the "squares" who made up the majority of the student population. When he wasn't getting beaten up, that is.

The doorbell rang, and Tillie glanced at the clock over the sink. "That would be your partner in crime," she said. "Time to get cracking."

With a quick goodbye Marnie scooped up her books and bolted out the front door into the muggy humidity where her best friend awaited.

"'Bout time, sleepyhead," teased Charlotte, attired in her customary conservative skirt and blouse. Her parents were quite active in the Baptist church Marnie and her father attended. Charlotte's dad also owned the local supermarket where the girls were to be employed this upcoming summer as cash register baggers. Like Marnie, she was slight of build (but blonde) and quite athletic, and the two frequently studied together to maintain their A- averages. They trusted each other with their secrets, and boys were a frequent topic.

However, though she was understanding of Marnie's preoccupation with the Beatles, the opinions of other less tolerant classmates bothered Charlotte, and more than once this past year she'd had to ask her best friend to tone it down a bit when she'd start expounding on the virtues of the Fab Four's music. "Y'all aren't ever gonna have boys ask you out if you spend all your time mooning over the Beatles," she'd recently counseled.

"I know, you're right," Marnie had answered. "I get carried away sometimes."

Today their conversation on the twenty-minute walk to school centered on report cards and summer plans. Both expected to do well academically and looked forward to the cookouts and outings at the lake that would commence with Memorial Day this coming weekend.

"You think Tommy Plummer will ask you out this weekend at the church picnic?" Marnie asked. "He's been making eyes at you this past month in English class."

"I think that's a good possibility," Charlotte said confidently. "I wouldn't mind going out with the future quarterback of the varsity, would you?"

"Guess not. It's just that he's, well, y'know, kinda—"

"Square? Clean cut? Is that it? Well, I'll be honest with you, I don't mind at all. He comes from a good family, who has lots of money, by the way. If he wants to spend some of it on this little girl, I'm not gonna stop him."

The two laughed.

"And what about Myles, Marnie? Do you like him?"

"We're just friends," she stated primly. "He's a good guy. The fact that he's Jewish doesn't mean much to me, though my dad probably wouldn't approve. Anyway, a girl can have guy friends, you know, without it being romantic."

"Still holding out for Paul?" Charlotte teased. "John's married, you know, with a son—"

"Will you *stop*, please? I just haven't met the right guy yet, Char. Maybe this summer."

"Yeah, Marnie, the possibilities will be *endless* at the checkout counter. Maybe Prince Charming will stop in for a can of tuna fish."

* * *

Even though the last day of school was only a half session, it was still a drag. Time to clean out lockers and say goodbye to one's friends and teachers for the summer. Of course, to keep a lid on the place the students' report cards were to be distributed in homeroom at the very end of the day. As expected, Marnie had gotten a B in math, her hardest subject, and As the rest of the way, which was one reason her dad went easy on her with the Beatles stuff. Still, The Sarge had no aspirations of a college career for his daughter. A secretarial job with some company—while she looked for a husband, of course—was more the norm in his world. It didn't matter that Marnie's mom had been a secretary as well, for the man she'd eventually run off with.

Marnie was tossing out the last of the old bagged lunches that had been decomposing in the bottom of her locker when she felt a familiar tap on the shoulder. Marnie had long since ceased to be spooked when Myles sneaked up on her. In fact, it was their usual way of saying hello.

"Wow, how old is *that* one?" he said, wrinkling his nose. "My guess is baloney and mayo."

"Close. It's ham," she replied, peeking inside for a second. "Or it *was*." Marnie noticed her friend looked a little out of sorts. "S'matter, Myles," she said, "you pull an F in science or something?"

"Uh, no," he answered, taking off his tortoise shell glasses for a quick polish.

"Somebody pickin' on you again?"

"Uh-uh, not today."

"Well, that's an improvement. So, what's up?"

He pulled an envelope from his back pocket and held it out, his face flushing red. "Uh, happy birthday," he said.

"It's not for another week, Myles."

"Yeah, I know, but I might not see you next week. Would you just open it?"

She frowned good-naturedly while tearing off the end. "Jeez Louise, Myles, you didn't have to get me a—"

"Careful!" he hissed.

She gave him a suspicious look, then slowly peeled off the rest of the envelope's corner and reached inside. There was, indeed, a card from the five and dime, simply signed *Hope you like it, Myles*. But it was what was *inside* the card that took her breath away: an orange cardboard ticket with red and black lettering for a Beatles concert to be held on Friday, August 19, at the Memphis Mid-South Coliseum at 8:30 PM. The price on the ticket was $5.50. Marnie, usually at no loss for words, was dumbstruck. "What…how…" was all she could manage.

Myles held up a hand to stop her. "It was just announced," he explained. "They're doing a foreign tour first, and then coming to the US. Well, as you know, my dad's pretty well-connected, so it was fairly easy for him—"

He never got to finish his explanation (which included the fact that he was the owner of a second ticket) because Marnie grabbed him around the waist and started twirling him in the semi-crowded hallway until they finally collapsed in a laughing heap on the beige linoleum floor.

If the Beatles had a birthday song, she would have sung it out loud.

Chapter Two

If Marnie Culpeper thought her junior high years had been tumultuous, she had nothing on the four Liverpudlians who called themselves the Beatles, in either scope or severity.

Together in their current lineup as a rock and roll combo since 1962, the band's roots went all the way back to the chance meeting of like-minded teenagers John Lennon and Paul McCartney at an outdoor church fete in Woolton, Liverpool in 1957. Though different in personality, the boys hit it off because they shared an ambitious—if somewhat unlikely—dream of becoming the next Elvis Presley. Both boys had lost their mothers at an early age, which further bonded them. And although they were different in personality—John being the rather cheeky teen that was the bane of any teacher's existence, while Paul came across as sincere, charming, and eager to please—they proved early on to be soulmates who would forge one of the closest, and most successful, partnerships in modern musical history.

* * *

Rock and roll, as it came to be known, was still in its relative infancy in the US, where it had evolved from rhythm and blues and jazz during the years following World War II. The earliest stars had been black, with Elvis coming in by the mid-50s along with such white luminaries as Jerry Lee Lewis, Roy Orbison, and Carl Perkins. This new, electric sound made its way to blue-collar port cities in England such as Liverpool by way of merchant seamen returning from the States with the much sought-after vinyl talismans of American culture: rock and roll records. Lennon and McCartney, halfhearted academics at best, began soaking up all they could about American popular music, forming the band that would come to include schoolmate George Harrison and, finally, flamboyant drummer Richie Starkey, whose stage moniker was the catchy Ringo Starr.

By the time they were "discovered" by future manager Brian Epstein in the dingy Cavern Club in Liverpool, where they had become local celebrities, the Beatles were a seasoned rock and roll band that had served an apprenticeship by fire in the rough and tumble clubs of Hamburg, Germany, and returned to England as a tight, energetic group with distinctive bowl-cut hairdos introduced to them by a female German friend.

Less than two years later, after signing with Epstein, the group had traded its leather "Teddy Boy" outfits for matching Edwardian suits and high heeled boots, put themselves in the trust of brilliant studio producer George Martin, who would act as both mentor and collaborator going forward, and secured a recording contract with a prominent record label. This in itself would have been dizzying enough for the four lads from Liverpool, but a string of hit records in the

UK led to tours in Western Europe, which featured large, enthusiastic crowds of screaming girls, the likes of which had never been seen in the British Isles. And then, in the wake of the tragic assassination of President John Fitzgerald Kennedy in November 1963, came the cracking of the Top 40 AM radio lists in the States, and an invitation to play on the greatest stage in American culture—an appearance on the Ed Sullivan variety show in February of 1964.

The phenomenon that would come to be known as "Beatlemania" had begun.

From New York the group conducted a whirlwind East Coast tour of indoor venues, including Washington and Miami, where they again appeared live on the Sullivan show, playing to now-shrieking capacity crowds, made up mostly of teenaged girls.

They returned to England at the end of February 1964 as conquering heroes, greeted at Heathrow Airport in London by thousands of their adoring UK fans, whose sense of national pride skyrocketed. It was incredible, really; never in the history of popular music had a British act so captivated not only their own country, but the United States, whose music the Beatles and everyone else had copied for years. The pop music industry was literally turned upside down.

But the Beatles, spurred on by both their own ambition, as well as the general consensus of the adult public that they were a passing fad destined to fizzle out, kept the pedal to the metal, beginning a spring UK tour in April that ended with a command performance for members of the Royal Family in which the cheeky John Lennon invited the regents to "rattle their jewelry" in time to the music.

As if their pace was not hectic enough, the group filmed their first movie, a semi-documentary entitled *A Hard Day's Night,* shot in black and white, that showcased not only their music (the movie would provide still more Top 40 hits, such as the title track, the bouncy "Can't Buy Me love," and "She Loves You," which featured the infectious "yeah, yeah, yeah" refrain that had kids everywhere singing along) but their irreverent and endearing Liverpudlian wit. Soon there would be teens lined up around the block for showing after showing, screaming their heads off for the duration of the film. Somehow, the boys managed to get themselves into the recording studio at Abbey Road in St. John's Wood in London, an upscale residential area where, under the guidance of Martin, they continued to crank out melodies—both romantic and rockers—that shot to the top of the charts.

By this time, anyone with a business sense could see the Beatles as a potential gold mine, and manager Epstein was besieged with hucksters pitching everything from Beatles tee shirts, hats and apparel, to Beatles buttons, lunch boxes, notebooks, wigs, and anything else they could affix the band's name to. Unfortunately, their harried manager was overwhelmed with this unprecedented explosion of pop-culture memorabilia, and many of the deals that were made garnered for the lads only a fraction of what might have been—and this was not even counting the thousands of "bootleg" items being offered for sale in various countries.

Epstein felt, and rightfully so, that the Beatles had to ride this towering wave of popularity that had yet to crest, and that live performances, in which they could showcase the multiple hits now in their repertoire, were the quickest path to continued financial success. Thus, it was time to think globally as far as the Beatles next frontier to explore; so, beginning in August of 1964, the Beatles set out to conquer the world, first landing in Copenhagen, then pressing on to Amsterdam, Hong Kong and Australia, with refueling stops in such outposts as Zürich, Beirut, Karachi, Calcutta, and Bangkok in between.

At each stop, be it for a concert or brief layover, the "Fab Four" were expected to submit to inane interviews and press conferences, while holed up in the penthouse suites of various hotels, prisoners of their burgeoning fame. Most of these they handled with the same aplomb and humor they had displayed at their first hastily put together event after their landing at New York's recently named JFK Airport back in February, where they had completely charmed the notoriously cynical New York media with their self-deprecating, clever comebacks. These guys were *funny!* But even the Fab Four, subjected to the continuous grind, showed times of weariness and annoyance that were inevitable for a group of 20-somethings thrust into a global spotlight.

When they could get out, they were, as Paul McCartney would say, "like dogs let off the leash." Fortunately, any wild or lurid stories of their exploits were kept from their adoring teenybopper fans, who mounted assaults on their temporary strongholds that would make Attila the Hun blush with envy. It was not uncommon for girls to try to smuggle themselves in using laundry hampers, bedsheets tied together from roofs as lowering devices, or death-defying tightrope walks along outside wall ledges. Here and there, to quell the madness, the boys would deign to appear on the hotel balcony, waving to the masses below, "like Caesars" as John Lennon put it.

But the Western European/Asian/Australian swing was just the beginning. After an all too brief respite, the band was off for the North American leg of their tour, crisscrossing the US and Canada, from the Cow Palace in San Francisco and the Hollywood Bowl in Los Angeles, to Maple Leaf Gardens and the Montréal Forum, to the Boston Garden and Paramount Theater on the East Coast.

They returned to the UK in September 1964, utterly exhausted but percolating with new Lennon-McCartney compositions that would keep them in the forefront of what was becoming known as the "British Invasion"—English bands like the Rolling Stones, Dave Clark Five, Herman's Hermits, and a host of others who followed in their trailblazing wake. Indeed, by the summer of '64 *anything* British was considered cool, especially in the States; even the Jaguar Motor Corporation saw sales of their classic XKE sports car take off.

But as the year came to a close (after yet another UK tour in autumn), the Beatles, sitting atop the entertainment world, famous and wealthy beyond their wildest dreams, could hardly imagine the changes awaiting them around the next corner, changes that would gradually transform them from the ebullient moptops of Marnie Culpeper's fantasies to the rapidly maturing and world-weary adults they would inevitably become.

Chapter Three

Living with The Sarge wasn't easy. Marnie's dad was a walking bundle of contradictions, his personality having been molded through a variety of life experiences, some tough times, and his profession.

Roy Culpeper cut an imposing figure. At 6 foot, 2 inches of rock-hard muscle, topped by a square head accentuated by a military issue crewcut, he gave off a somewhat threatening aura that commanded immediate respect. And when he donned his Memphis PD sergeant's uniform, with its blue pants, short-sleeved white shirt and tie, spit-shined black shoes buffed to a mirror finish, topped with a blue-visored hat, he was positively intimidating.

But Marnie knew there were many layers below the surface of her father, and that few people—including his police force brothers, good ol' boy friends, and certainly his ex-wife—really understood him. Even Marnie found him infuriating and distant at times, and as she entered her mid-teens, only now was she starting to get a handle on what made the big guy tick. As far as she could tell, there were two things that had shaped her father as a man: growing up poor, and his service in the Korean War.

Roy's childhood had been a hardscrabble one,

with his family of seven living off his father's paycheck from a local sawmill in rural Western Tennessee. The two boys in the brood, Roy and his older brother Jimmy, had worked picking cotton for pennies a day, most days until their hands bled. Any meager pay they received had been immediately deposited in the family pot. Most of the time there was food on the table, especially during hunting season, when Joe Culpeper would take his boys out for deer, ducks or pheasant. But living conditions in their two-room tarpaper shack were primitive. Roy would not use a proper bathroom facility until his first posting at a US military training base.

This grim upbringing instilled in Roy an abject fear of being poor, and he vowed as a young man that if he were given the opportunity to have his own family, he would drastically improve their standard of life from the squalor in which he had been raised. And he would always use his money wisely, not throwing it away on whisky, women, or gambling, as so many of his father's friends seemed to do. Roy's only vice was an occasional cigarette or cigar which he'd enjoy when out hunting or fishing with his friends, like-minded blue-collar men with names like Tee Bob and Billie Ray.

His time overseas, however, had affected him in far deeper, more subtle ways. As a twenty-year-old high school graduate and current employee at the very sawmill where his father worked, Roy, as well as his brother, had jumped at the chance to serve his country and escape the humdrum but dangerous existence of a mill worker. (His father had been declared unfit for service in World War II because of the loss of a finger in the sawmill.) And so, the Culpeper boys went off to fight the communists in North

Korea. It wasn't long before Roy began to show an aptitude for leadership that his laconic older brother lacked, and by the time they had completed their basic infantry training at Fort Hood, Texas, he was already being considered for a promotion in rank.

But although combat duty was what Roy had been hoping for, the brutal conditions that his unit found themselves in—especially the freezing winter months in North Korea—quickly soured him on the glories of war. As predicted, his cool-headedness and courage in battle—accompanied by the heavy losses incurred by his unit—saw him reach the rank of sergeant rather quickly. However, during the winter of 1950 campaign, his 8th Cavalry unit was thrown into a virtual meat grinder, and Roy Culpeper witnessed horrors that would change him forever. When word got to him that Jimmy was missing in action, Roy had begun to wonder when his own number would come up.

On November 20, 1950, it did.

That frosty morning, Roy was walking point on a patrol near Unsan when his platoon was ambushed by the enemy. They radioed for help and dug in, for many hours fending off a superior enemy force while absorbing staggering losses. Roy was crawling towards a wounded comrade who was crying for his mother when a North Korean machine gun round tore into his left shoulder. Unable to stanch the flow of blood, Roy blacked out, and didn't wake up until he was flat on his back in a MASH unit behind the lines.

"Congratulations," said the surgeon visiting his bedside. "You're going home with a million-dollar wound, Sarge." A Purple Heart medal was pinned to his pillow.

"H-how did I get here?" he rasped, trying to sit up.

"Easy, boy, we don't want to open up that thing again. You lost a lot of blood," cautioned the surgeon. "From what I was told, your platoon held the fort until some artillery could be laid down on the commies. Then, one of your men hefted you over his shoulder and carried you for over a mile to the rear, where they helicoptered you out. You've been here for about a week now. For a while it was touch and go."

"Who carried me back?" inquired Roy.

"Apparently, that colored boy to your left in the next cot."

Roy painfully turned his head to see the image of Pfc. Leroy Washington, hooked up to an IV drip and apparently in a deep sleep. That a colored man would risk his life for a Southern cracker like himself touched the hard-bitten sergeant so deeply he couldn't speak at first. Then, he managed to croak, "Did he get hit, too? He doesn't look too bad."

"Except that one of his legs is missing, Sarge," said the surgeon with a sigh. "That boy carried you a mile with half his lower right leg shot away. It's pretty incredible, when you think about it."

"Is... he gonna make it?"

The surgeon frowned. "We're having a problem getting an infection under control. We'll see."

Then Roy passed out. The next day when Roy woke up, Washington was gone, his cot occupied by a different soldier.

Roy Culpeper recovered from his wound and returned home to little fanfare. The Korean "police action" his country was involved in still had some time to run and was currently in a stalemate. There would be no victory parades across the country as was the case in 1945, and the conflict would fade into history. But not for Roy, who on many nights would continue to be haunted by the sounds of exploding shells and screaming men, causing him to awaken with a start, his bed sheets sodden with sweat.

Once stateside and fully recovered from his injuries, it was time for Roy to decide what he wanted to do with the rest of his life, and his decision was quick; he wanted a career in law enforcement. To that end, he applied, and was accepted, into the Memphis Police Department training program, where he excelled, graduating at the top of his class.

At the same time, he began courting a girl named Maybelle Miller, whom he'd met at a church social. Maybelle was pretty and perky and loved to go out dancing, which was fine with Roy. And though she didn't share his interests in hunting and fishing, she wasn't averse to him having his own friends and hobbies. The two enjoyed each other's company and soon married, purchasing a tidy, newly built home in Memphis on the G.I. Bill and settling in to a relatively happy, routine life. With Roy's salary from Memphis PD and Maybelle's as a secretary, they did all right, and usually managed a night out on the weekend. Their first child, named Marnie after Roy's deceased mother, came along in June 1951, and it appeared the young couple had everything they could want.

But the seemingly idyllic marriage of Roy and Maybelle started showing cracks not long after Marnie's toddler years. Now encumbered with a child to look after, Maybelle began to ask for outside help in the home, a notion that the old-fashioned Roy could not fathom. And when they did hire Tillie, the mistress of the house was not as quick to come home after work; nor did she feel the urge to pick up the slack with any domestic chores that Tillie couldn't get to. More and more, Roy and his wife found themselves plopping on the couch when he wasn't on the late shift and watching TV. And when Tillie didn't have time to prepare a meal before she left in the late afternoon, Maybelle invariably heated up a Swanson TV dinner for her husband. Their life together became a grind, exacerbated by his bouts of depression brought on by the war.

The only light Roy's eyes, then, was his daughter.

Marnie's early years had been marked by trips with her daddy to the local playground, where he pushed her to dizzying heights on the swings and watched her scramble on the monkey bars. He patiently taught her how to ride a bike and "throw like a boy" when playing catch in their neat, postage stamp-sized backyard. Then, when she was a little older, there were overnight camping trips to nearby Pickwick Lake, where she was versed in how to pitch a tent, start a fire, and bait a fishhook. They would catch a few catfish; clean, filet and bread them, and cook them in butter in an iron skillet while the sun went down. Sometimes during these activities Marnie wondered if her father had really wanted a son, but if he did he never let on. Unfortunately, her mom was not interested in sports or outdoorsy stuff. But that was okay with Marnie. She treasured this time alone with her dad, who would crack open a beer or two as they sat by the campfire and, here and there, share a little about his life experiences. Except the war. *Never* the war.

But after JFK died and Mom left, something had

come over her father, something sad and ominous. During their shared, home-cooked dinners that Tillie had prepared, including such favorites as country ham with red-eye gravy, Memphis-style cornbread salad and coleslaw, and lemon ice box pie, her dad could become withdrawn, with one-syllable responses the norm. He still was interested in school and whatever else was going on in her life (although he gave boys a wide berth), but it wasn't the same as those earlier campouts, which were becoming less frequent. As 1966 rolled around, Roy Culpeper was content to come home from his shift, having changed into civilian clothes back at headquarters, eat his dinner—now frequently accompanied by one or two Budweisers—and settle into his La-Z-Boy for a night of TV. Marnie even knew his viewing schedule:

Monday: *The Iron Horse* and *The Rat Patrol*

Tuesday: *Combat!* and *The Red Skelton Hour*

Wednesday: *The Virginian* and *Gomer Pyle, USMC*

Friday: *The Wild, Wild West* and *Hogan's Heroes*

Saturday: *The Jackie Gleason Show* and *Mission: Impossible*

Sunday: *Voyage to the Bottom of the Sea* and *Bonanza*

Because there was only one TV in the house, Marnie did manage to coax a few shows out of her dad, such as *Walt Disney's Wonderful World of Color, I Dream of Jeannie,* and *Flipper.* Thursday, especially, was "her night," with *Batman, Bewitched,* and occasionally, *The Dating Game,* which she could tell her dad thought was stupid.

Obviously, her father's tastes ran to Westerns,

action shows and war-themed vehicles. Especially disconcerting was the tendency of Roy, usually after another couple Budweisers, to tear up during *Combat!* He would even mutter at the TV on occasion, stuff like "That's how it was," or "Good move, Sarge," referring to the show's protagonist, the gruff but caring Sgt. Saunders, played by Vic Morrow. It was during these times that Marnie would look up from her homework materials that were splayed on the living room carpet and ask, "You okay, Daddy?"

To which he would invariably reply, "Sure thing, darlin'. Want to fetch me another beer?"

Her father's detachment, of course, allowed Marnie to pursue her hobby of the Beatles, which Roy seldom asked about. Oh, he might venture into her room and cluck his tongue at the decorations, the map on her cork board which was studded with different color-headed sewing pins that tracked the various tours the group had undertaken, and of course Myles's record player contraption (the installation of which Tillie had to supervise, while Marnie waited in the living room), but that was the extent of his interest.

Marnie wished her dad would go out more besides the occasional hunting or fishing trip with his buddies. There were many women at their church who cast an eye Roy's way as he and his daughter—who always wore a dress on Sunday, as per his orders— entered the First Baptist Church. But outside of the occasional church function, such as the annual Memorial Day picnic, Roy kept a low profile.

Deep down, Marnie wondered if what was currently going on in the world—especially the increasing involvement of US forces in Vietnam and the intensifying Civil Rights Movement—were having an effect on her dad's well-being. They rarely discussed either issue, but Marnie could tell when they watched the evening news that the images of soldiers trudging through the jungles of Vietnam, which seemed to be a hot, steamy, godforsaken place, had a negative effect on him. But, was he for or against our participation? She knew he was anti-communist, as evidenced by his willingness to participate in the Korean War, which, like this one, was conducted in the hopes of containing communism, but that was it.

As for the civil rights thing, he would stonily watch the images of Southern black and white confrontations, including clips of policemen in Alabama using fire hoses and snarling dogs to repel protesting Negroes seeking the rights to ride at the front of buses and share restrooms, water fountains, and lunch counters with whites. Clearly, these scenes were wearing on him. She imagined he was conflicted over having a Negro woman in his employ, though he could barely afford it. She also wondered if there were events in his murky past that had helped to shape his view on this increasingly volatile topic. But above all, Marnie feared for his safety as he performed what appeared to be his solemn duty to protect and serve the citizens of Memphis, Tennessee— no matter their color.

Chapter Four

As the Beatles entered 1965, they hardly paid attention to the question constantly posed to them: When will the bubble burst? There was too much going on to even think about it. Their records had flooded Top 40 charts and department store shelves everywhere. *A Hard Day's Night* was still raking in money at the box office, and they were greeted with staggering crowds of adoring fans no matter where they appeared. Even they agreed that it was all crazy, and that they were simply an excuse for the world to go mad. And even though they publicly pooh-poohed the idea of being role models to the current generation of teens, there was no getting around it. Everything they did, said, or sang was now being scrutinized.

Personal appearances in the form of concerts were becoming downright dicey, with even the beefed-up security forces employed by most venues proving inadequate against the surging masses. The group would take to the stage after they'd been driven to the concert hall in some kind of armored car or heavy truck, clutching their guitars to their chests like shields. They'd go through a breakneck half hour show of roughly eleven songs while flashbulbs exploded and girls wept or shrieked until many fainted dead away and had to be carried off. With their still primitive amplifiers and the poor sound systems of most concert venues, the boys could barely hear themselves or stay in rhythm, not that it mattered. Then it was on to the airport, another hotel, and the concert madness all over again.

But the year 1965 saw the beginnings of the Fab Four distancing themselves from their lovable moptop image, in a subtle variety of ways, unnoticed by their fans. Most notably was their experimentation with drugs.

As typical blue-collar Brits, the Beatles had grown up in and around the pub culture held so dear by the English. Stopping off for a pint after a long day's work to socialize with local friends was, and still is, a cherished ritual in the UK. And so, it was normal for the boys, going back to their teen years, to enjoy a few beers wherever they might be (later to be augmented with such rudimentary mixed drinks as rum or scotch blended with Coca-Cola).

The Beatles' first experience with drugs had come during their Hamburg days, where they were forced to play until all hours in seedy nightclubs, most times doing two shows a day. To stay awake and remain sharp, they started taking Preludin, an amphetamine that kept them on their toes when they should have been sleeping. But as far as recreational drugs were concerned, there were none as such in their lives until a meeting with one of their musical idols would change all that.

The group was into its 1965 US tour, which began with a record-breaking August 15 appearance at Shea Stadium, the brand-new home of the New York Mets baseball team. The hysteria for this occasion had built to the point that the band had to be helicoptered into the steaming cauldron of 55,000 screaming teens, thus ushering in the concept of athletic stadium concerts. And although the Beatles' equipment was woefully inadequate for the size of the venue, nobody seemed to mind. Positioned on a stage erected behind second base, the group tore through such fan favorites as "Twist and Shout," "I Feel Fine," "Can't Buy Me Love" and "A Hard Day's Night" as teenagers and women cried, screamed, passed out, or tried to break through the ring of NYPD security to rush the stage. It was complete chaos, and at the same time, totally exhilarating. The Beatles had climbed the Mount Everest of live performances.

It was while they were in New York that folksinger Bob Dylan, who had certainly influenced the songwriting members of the group, most notably John Lennon, dropped in for a momentous visit. After getting over their starstruck awkwardness (much the same as they would display in a meeting with Elvis Presley later during the tour), the Beatles accepted from Dylan the offer of marijuana joints and were quite pleased with its effects. It seemed the perfect antidote for the craziness that surrounded them at all times, and they became avid users, though never on stage.

Thus, when Marnie Culpeper and her friends found themselves sitting through multiple screenings of the Beatles' second film, *Help!*, they had no way of knowing that the movie, which was filmed in such diverse locales as the Austrian Alps and the Bahamas, was done so through a haze of marijuana that made it difficult for the boys to memorize their lines and led to fits of giggles that frustrated the production crew.

The movie itself was a bit silly, or at least its

premise. Taking advantage of the current popularity of the James Bond films—something that the Beatles' stardom as Britons had helped promote—the plot revolved around problems encountered by the band when Ringo inadvertently received a ring in the mail from a fan in some far Eastern country, which he decided to wear. The problem was, the ring was part of a ritualistic sacrificial ceremony in this country and was one of a kind. Immediately, fanatical holy men were dispatched to England to bring back the ring—which had become inextricably stuck on the drummer's finger—even if it meant killing poor Ringo and all his mates, who were considered heathens for their barbaric music. These zealots were later joined by a mad scientist who saw the power of the ring and wanted it for himself. By the time it all got sorted out, Scotland Yard and even the British Army had become involved to protect the Beatles from harm as they hopped from one country to another evading their pursuers—while, of course, stopping here and there to perform a handful of new hits, including the title track, "Ticket to Ride," and others that would be worked into the 1965 summer tour's repertoire.

The director of the film, who had also done the classic "A Hard Day's Night" a year earlier, tried to stick to the game plan of having the boys deliver rapid fire one-liners rather than have to do any real acting. But the result, as noted in film reviews, came up a little short of its predecessor. Not that it mattered; *Help!* made money hand over fist, and Marnie surely did her share to help the cause.

After Shea Stadium, the Beatles settled into the familiar double-time pace of concerts throughout

August in a combination of hockey, baseball, and football arenas, the lone nonsporting venue the Hollywood Bowl in Los Angeles. They returned to England exhausted, the grind of touring wearing on them more each time they ventured from their homeland. But even back in England, there was always another local appearance, either live or on the BBC, or a television taping or press conference to attend to. It was incredible that despite being pulled in so many directions—with even a pause to receive a medal from the Queen for all they had done to promote Great Britain abroad—the Beatles could find the time to record that next hit single or album to keep the airwaves humming with their music. But Lennon and McCartney seemed to be an endless font of tunes, and when the group convened at Abbey Road studios in the fall of 1965 to begin work on their new LP, the influences on the band gathered throughout the year would come together to produce a different kind of Beatles album in which the group would begin a departure from the typical boy/girl romantic themes of the past three years. The Beatles were rapidly maturing musically, and would inevitably drag their fan base, including Marnie Culpeper, who still watched Beatles cartoons every Saturday morning, along for the ride.

Chapter Five

In early December 1965 Marnie got a call that both intrigued her and made her jealous. Myles had acquired a copy of the brand-new Beatles album entitled *Rubber Soul*.

"You lucky dog," she said wistfully. "I'll have to wait until Christmas to get mine."

"That doesn't mean you can't come over and give it a listen," Myles said playfully.

"You mean it? I'll be right over!" she cried. After giving her hair a quick brushing, she was out the door in an instant and pedaling her Schwinn the mile or so to the Goldfarbs' house.

"Estate" was more like it. Myles's dad was a well-to-do businessman who had been transferred from New York a few years earlier. And although Mr. Goldfarb had appeared to adapt well to Memphis (though he traveled quite a bit), Mrs. Goldfarb didn't seem too keen on the move. Marnie could sense that she considered the South backward, and the fact that they had virtually no Jewish friends probably made her feel even more isolated and out of place. And when the Goldfarbs did try to get into the swing of things by applying for membership to an exclusive country club on the outskirts of town, they were mysteriously turned down.

It wasn't any easier for their only child at school. Between his distinctive New York accent and ethnicity—not to mention his gawky stature and mannerisms—Myles was subjected to almost constant harassment by his classmates, especially the boys, who considered him effeminate, though he most certainly was interested in girls. Marnie, being the goodhearted soul she was, immediately gravitated towards him, and the two became fast friends, though neither Myles's mom nor The Sarge were thrilled about it.

Myles was a builder and a thinker whose inquisitive mind and talent for scientific deduction made him shine in school—except in English, where creative writing was a chore for him. Since this was Marnie's very strength, the two of them often studied together, leading to whispers at school that they were secretly going steady. But the two had reached an understanding of sorts that their friendship would remain platonic, and that any attempt to take it further would only result in the kind of fleeting disasters encountered by their classmates as they navigated the waters of adolescent romance.

Besides academics, the two would also get together at a nearby public tennis court to volley back and forth while they discussed the matters of the day, whether it be the goings-on at school, Marnie's love life, world events, or their greatest common denominator—the Beatles.

Myles was somewhat of a rock and roll aficionado, having brought with him to Memphis a huge collection of LPs and 45s, as well as a formidable stereo system his parents had installed in their spacious living room. Marnie had the feeling that because Mr. Goldfarb was rarely around and his mother wasn't a touchy-feely person, they substituted material things as symbols of affection for their only child. Quite frankly, listening to music over at Myles's house was like being at a concert, as opposed to Marnie's rudimentary bedroom phonograph set up. So, to be able to give the Beatles' new album a listen on Myles's multi-speaker rig was a real treat. But even more, the two were able to discuss the music on a far more intelligent level from that of their classmates at school, whose ratings on songs rarely went beyond the American Bandstand kind of evaluations based on catchiness of the beat and danceability.

She pulled into the long Goldfarb driveway that led to a white mock-antebellum building with Greek columns which stood out even in this upscale neighborhood. Myles met her at the side door and excitedly ushered her inside. "Where's your mom?" Marnie asked.

"Out back on the patio, reading," he replied, "and maybe having a drink."

"At one in the afternoon?"

"Yeah, well…" he answered with a shrug, his voice trailing off.

Marnie decided to let it drop. "Let's see the cover," she said, sinking into the living room's deep pile carpet, surrounded by speakers in every corner of the tastefully decorated room. What she saw shocked her. A few seconds had to pass before the girl managed, "They look different."

"Well, *that's* an understatement," he said.

Unlike previous album covers that captured the boys' moptop cuteness, the Beatles who stared out at

Marnie looked sad, even morose, and it seemed that something had been done to the camera lens so their faces appeared elongated. None of them wore suits and ties, and the only lettering on the cover were the words *Rubber Soul* in a puffy, somewhat inflated font. Marnie wondered, with some alarm, if the music contained inside would reflect a similar departure to the norm.

It did.

In the group's previous half-dozen albums, not to mention their standard 45s, it always seemed the Beatles were speaking directly to her. Whether it was in catchy tunes like "From Me to You," "I'm Happy Just to Dance with You," "I Want to Hold Your Hand," or romantic ballads such as "And I Love Her," "If I Fell," or most recently, "Yesterday," Marnie felt a visceral connection to the musicians, a sense that they really understood how a girl like her felt about love and romance.

The songs on this disc, though, although again centered on the themes of love and relationships, were more introspective and deep. Maybe it was because most of them featured acoustic guitar play and could in no way be considered "danceable." Or maybe it was the addition of such exotic instruments as a bouzouki, sitar and fuzz bass. Myles, the more musically educated of the two, had to point them out when, for example, she blurted out, "What in the Sam Hill is *that?*" during the opening sitar strains of "Norwegian Wood."

The lyrics were especially perplexing to the girl. Rather than the "yeah, yeah, yeah" and "woo-oo" chants of earlier songs, these compositions featured themes of unrequited love and disillusionment, whether it was in "You Won't See Me," "Think for Yourself," or "I'm Looking Through You." Though there were some truly beautiful cuts such as "Michelle," "It's Only Love," and "In My Life," Marnie was left with a sense that the game had changed for the Beatles, and it wasn't until the pair of teens had listened to the album three straight times that she even offered an appraisal.

"It's really good," she ventured haltingly, "but I'm not sure I get it all."

"That pretty much sums it up for me as well," Myles said. "It's just that, I don't know, could you see any of these songs being real hits? Or the Beatles playing them on TV or live? I don't know if they'd go over too well."

"Yeah, you may be right," she said.

As Marnie pedaled home that afternoon, she replayed over and over what she'd heard in Myles's living room and contemplated what it all meant. Which is why what happened next was so incongruous, though strangely comforting. As she approached her back door, she could see, through its glass panes, Tillie hard at work ironing one of The Sarge's uniforms. Nothing out of the ordinary there. But on the kitchen counter sat Tillie's transistor radio, blaring "Twist and Shout" from the previous year, and the housekeeper was actually twisting along to it as she pressed the clothes. Rather than surprise the woman and have her harrumph away her actions, Marnie made a production of clomping on the side steps and jiggling open the door knob so Tillie had time to gather herself.

Marnie entered the kitchen to hear the woman muttering her usual, "Sinful, sinful, sinful" mantra. Then she looked up. "Where you been, Miss Marnie?"

"Over at Myles Goldfarb's house," Marnie

replied, trying to mask a smile. "We were listening to the new Beatles album."

Tillie jerked a finger towards the transistor radio, from which the last strident strains of the song were emanating. "Hope they've come up with something different than *that*," she said.

You have no idea, thought Marnie.

Chapter Six

If 1965 revealed hints that the Beatles were changing, the following year would make it obvious, leaving their fans disappointed, exhilarated, or just plain confused.

By the time January of 1966 had ended, three of the four were married, with Paul the lone holdout. Some had also begun to explore other areas of interest beyond music, with George Harrison, through his fascination with Indian music and the sitar, becoming immersed in Eastern religion, Paul McCartney thoroughly embracing the London art scene and John Lennon, having already published a book of poems and art entitled *In His Own Write*, signing on to play a supporting role in an upcoming dark comedy about World War II. They had also moved on from their open acceptance of marijuana to the occasional sampling of stronger drugs, all done in an effort to become more creative as individual artists and musicians. Of course, this was kept from their young fans and their parents, who frowned upon scenes from their first two movies that had pictured the boys smoking cigarettes.

What could *not* be kept from their fans, despite the best efforts of Brian Epstein, were the Beatles' views on world events. As de facto leaders of the young generation, they were constantly peppered with questions regarding such hot button topics as civil rights and segregation in America, and the deepening war in Vietnam. Although Paul McCartney continued to play the role of suave diplomat when pressed on these issues, it was clear to see that his songwriting partner was chafing under the figurative muzzle that had been placed on him. The always brutally honest and mouthy John Lennon was a ticking time bomb.

Musically, the group kept rolling. Despite its departure from the typical Beatles LP formula, *Rubber Soul* had sold over 1.2 million copies in its first nine days, a record-breaking amount. It was also influencing other songwriters of the day, most notably Brian Wilson of the Beach Boys, to step up their game and broaden their horizons. *Pet Sounds*, the California band's landmark album, would be released later that year.

As the Beatles cast an eye toward the inevitable upcoming tour schedule for the year, it almost appeared that they had become two separate entities musically: the rock and rollers who would tear through their old numbers and favorite covers of American songs while on stage, and the serious studio musicians they were yearning to become. When it was decided early on that there would not be a third Beatles movie—due mostly to the fact that a feasible script palatable to both the group and Epstein could not be found—their manager started laying the groundwork for a spring/summer touring schedule, while the boys retreated to Abbey Road studios in the winter of 1966, after some much-needed R & R, to begin work on the new LP.

It was clear straight away that musical evolution of the group was continuing when Paul presented to his bandmates not a love song, but the sad tale of a lonely spinster and her parish priest, which would evolve into "Eleanor Rigby," a number that would feature not electric guitars or Ringo's backing drums, but a string quartet. Another track, "For No One," examined the life of the girl who had ended a relationship and was moving on with her life. George Harrison's "Taxman" decried the crippling tax levies that the English government placed upon its subjects, especially those in the Beatles' tax bracket, and "Love You To" was a full on Indian-styled song that featured sitars, table and tambura. John Lennon continued his trend of looking inward for inspiration in his songs, something he had begun with "Help!" in 1965. Songs like "She Said She Said" were based on personal experiences and had nothing to do with romance or teen relationships. Even Ringo's infectious sing-along tune "Yellow Submarine," which would become a children's favorite, described a magical kingdom unlike any presented in pop/rock music to that date. But probably the greatest departure on the album, the one that heralded the Beatles' ascension to a higher plane of creativity, was the final track, "Tomorrow Never Knows."

This song seemed to summarize the theme of the new LP, namely that although love songs had their place—the gentle, Beach Boy-like "Here, There, and Everywhere," for example—the Beatles were going outside the norm to explore styles and themes that interested them. For "Tomorrow Never Knows," Lennon drew upon a text of Tibetan Buddhism,

Eastern religious chants, random tape loops spliced together, studio effects that altered his voice, and a bit of drug-induced enlightenment to create a piece that really featured only one musical chord. But it was so intricately layered—and aided by an almost hypnotic drum beat provided by the always underestimated Ringo—that the listener found himself transported to some mountaintop in the Himalayas, accompanying the Beatles in their search for the meaning of life, or some abstract notion.

Of course, the Beatles knew that with this album—most notably the final track—their music would pretty much cease to be viable in a concert setting, for the studio enhancements that they had worked out with George Martin could never be duplicated on stage, and this was fine with them. The group had grown so disillusioned with the screaming, the throwing of jellybeans (after Ringo had inadvertently mentioned in an interview that he enjoyed eating them), the poor acoustics, the isolation of sterile hotels, and the general madness that followed them everywhere on the road, that the concept of becoming a full-time studio band seemed increasingly appealing. Still, their live performances made boatloads of money for the boys, and so it was in March of 1966 during the visit to New York that Brian Epstein announced the Beatles' tentative tour schedule for the year, which included Europe, the Far East, and North America. Specifically, Japan was a huge record-buying market that the Beatles had yet to visit. Germany had played a crucial role in the group's early development (they had not returned since their climb to fame), and America was a virtual goldmine.

But although the spring and summer would present some "firsts" for the group, there would also be some notable "lasts."

For example, on May 1, the Beatles were on the bill to participate in what had become a yearly event for them: the NME Pollwinner's Concert, held at the Empire Pool at Wembley in North London. This concert would feature what the general public considered the best in British entertainment, with recognized winners in the rock and roll division performing a few choice numbers. This year's lineup included, among others, the Who, the Yardbirds, and the Rolling Stones. The Beatles, of course, would wrap up the show, and they didn't disappoint. Attired in dark suits and turtlenecks, they performed a 15-minute set which included "I Feel Fine," "If I Needed Someone," "I'm Down," and their current singles "Nowhere Man" and "Day Tripper." It seemed to be just another triumphant performance for the lads before their adoring British fans. No one could have imagined that it would be their last organized live concert on British soil.

Chapter Seven

Roy Culpeper wasn't one to bring his work home with him. Although his daughter was sure that he'd witnessed more than his share of robberies, homicides, and other unpleasant events in his daily rounds, he didn't share much with the teen, nor did she ask him to. But there were nights where he was more distant than others, and she wondered, in light of what was happening in the administration of law enforcement throughout the South, if it was becoming too much for him to bear.

This came into focus one Saturday morning in late March when Marnie, attired in work clothes and her well-worn orange Tennessee Volunteers ballcap, was mowing the lawn in front of her house. A beat-up Rambler pulled into the driveway with its windows rolled down, country music blaring from inside. The car's occupant was Cecil Blevins, a patrolman on the force whom The Sarge had taken under his wing. Cecil was kind of wiry, with a receding hairline and a doughy face only a mother could love, but he was by her father's account a diligent, methodical lawman who gave the taxpayers of Memphis an honest day's work. Cecil, a bachelor, also shared Roy's interest for the outdoors, often accompanying him on fishing or hunting expeditions when both had a free weekend day.

"Hidy, Punkin'," he said, unfolding his frame from the compact car. "Y'all still wearin' that raggedy Vols cap in public?"

She switched off the lawnmower, which sputtered, blew out a puff of blue smoke, and went silent. Removing the cap, she swept a shirtsleeve across her forehead and said, "Don't see why not, Cecil. If you need to be reminded, my team went 8-1-2 last season, with a trip to the Bluebonnet Bowl. So, this ol' cap is very comfortable on me, thank you."

"Well, you just wait," said Cecil, who originally hailed from Alabama, "I think Bear Bryant might have the final say in the SEC this year. Remember, the most you could do was get a tie with us last year, and this year we've got Kenny Stabler returning at quarterback."

Marnie remembered well the game at UT's Neyland Stadium that she and her dad, a rabid Vols fan, had attended despite it being played in a driving rainstorm. "Yeah, well, time will tell, Cecil," she said. "I wouldn't get too overconfident."

He sighed. "If you say so. Is your daddy around?"

"Yeah, he's downstairs in the basement, waiting for y'all."

"That's fine," said the man, removing a long canvas slipcase from the back seat of the car. "We're going to be cleaning our rifles for the upcoming season. Gonna bag us a bunch of turkeys, you bet."

"What fun," she retorted sarcastically. "Well, if you'll excuse me, I'll get back to business here." She reached for the mower's pull cord.

He held up a hand, which stopped her cold. "Hey, uh, before you crank that baby up, has your dad said anything to you about work lately?"

"Not really. Anything specific you're thinking about?"

Cecil put the rifle case in the crook of his arm and moved closer to her, so he could speak quietly. "You know, he's had some run-ins lately with the lieutenant."

Marnie frowned. Roy Culpeper clearly disliked his superior, Joe Bob Sutter. He felt that the lieutenant had risen to his rank in the department because of who he knew. Unlike her dad, Lt. Sutter was fleshy, with slits for eyes and a weak chin. He also had a weird, wine-colored birthmark along his left jawline that gave him a kind of menacing look. The first time Marnie had met him, at a police picnic, she had recoiled in horror until her father had explained it was a perfectly natural occurrence. Still, it creeped her out. And, if her dad was to be believed, Sutter wasn't much of a lawman, either. Rather, he was a politician who was as changeable as the wind and looking for any opportunity to curry favor with the department commander. More than once he'd intimated to Roy that his goal was to be the chief of the Memphis PD, and that if Roy wanted to climb the ladder with him he'd have to toe the line on Sutter's policies, as many of the younger patrolmen hired since Sutter made lieutenant had learned to do. Cecil was one of the few who gravitated toward The Sarge, which had not gone unnoticed by Sutter, which could explain why he was given some of the worst shift schedules and territories within the Memphis city limits. And although he was too proud to admit it, Marnie was sure her dad was getting stuck with a lot of the dirty work as well.

"What do you think is the problem, Cecil?" she

asked. "You know my dad, he won't say much to me, but I worry about him."

"So do I, Punkin'. I think a lot of it is this civil rights stuff. Sutter is a hardline segregationist; believe me, he woulda been right at home in Birmingham turnin' the fire hoses on the Nigras, and maybe worse. There's even rumors the guy is connected to the Klan." He whispered the last word as if its very utterance unnerved him.

"The KKK is inside the *police department?*" she said incredulously. "C'mon, Cecil, I think your imagination's gettin' the best of you."

"Listen, Punkin'," he said, still in whisper mode, "you're a youngster, so you don't see what I do. The Klan has members from every walk of life in its ranks. Don't you for a second think they're just piney woods rednecks. There's some guys in the Klan leadership with a lot of clout in these parts. Your daddy might not be a civil rights crusader like that King guy over in Alabama, but I think he's at least reasonable, and has a conscience. What I'm saying is, y'all keep an eye on him, and if it seems like he's in a deep hole, give me a holler."

She was nodding as Roy came bursting through the front door. "Cecil, you got any concept of time? Boy, you're at least a half-hour late. Are we gonna clean these guns or not?"

"Sure thing, Sarge," he said, jogging double-time towards the house, but not before he'd shot a wink at Marnie, who had to process what he'd said. She stood still for a few minutes, mulling over his words, then started up the mower again with a violent yank.

* * *

The following Monday, Marnie had shocked Tillie by turning up a full thirty minutes ahead of normal for breakfast. The housekeeper hadn't even had to yell for her to wake up. Sitting down to her morning meal of grits and honey, the girl asked nervously, "Uh, Tillie, can I talk to you about something for a minute?"

The woman stopped washing the previous evening's silverware and arched an eyebrow. "You got a problem, Miss Marnie?" she asked suspiciously. "Some boy stuff goin' on at the junior high?"

"No, nothing like that," the girl said reassuringly. "It's, uh, about my dad."

Tillie put her dishrag over the vertically aligned plates in the drying rack and sat down at the table, her hands folded before her. "Okay, I'm listening."

Marnie cleared her throat. "I've gotta ask you some things," she began, "things I've been thinking about all weekend."

"Do tell," said the housekeeper. "Well, go ahead, get it out."

"Okay. Tillie, how much do you talk to my dad, I mean *really* talk to him?"

The woman sighed. "Your daddy is a man of few words, even in the best of times. Fact is, we only cross paths sometimes at the very beginning or the very end of my work day. Sometimes we chat a bit when he's able to give me a ride home after work. Why? What is it you're getting at, honey?"

"Has he ever talked to you about, you know, the whole civil rights thing?"

A look came over the housekeeper that Marnie felt indicated she'd ventured into uncomfortable territory. "Tillie," she continued quietly, "I've paid attention to what-all's been going on down here the past few years. Those Freedom Rider people getting murdered, and the little girls in Birmingham who died in the church bombing, and the lunch counter sit-ins in Greensboro—"

"Why are you troubling yourself with all this?" said the woman. "You got enough to worry about just living your own life and taking care of your daddy."

"Because it *does* affect me," the girl countered. "Don't you think I wonder why our schools here are fighting integration like crazy? And why there's no colored kids in my whole junior high? And why your kids have to go to all-Negro schools on the other side of town? Good grief, Tillie, you've been with us for goin' on five years, and I hardly know anything about you!"

The woman pursed her lips, her face otherwise impassive. "That's just the way things are down here," she explained. "Do I like it? Of course not. My grandparents, and my husband's grandparents were slaves, and our parents were sharecroppers, which wasn't a whole lot better. But I like working for y'all; your family has always treated me right, and with respect, though I do think that what your momma did was just plain wrong. Still, what does this have to do with your daddy?"

"Tillie, this weekend a patrolman named Cecil Blevins, who works with Daddy, came by to see him, and he told me that things aren't too good at police headquarters."

"In what way?"

"Because of Lieutenant Sutter, daddy's boss."

"Oh, *him,*" she said, her brow furrowing.

"You know about Sutter?"

"Child, you could say he's somewhat well-known around town, and for all the wrong reasons. Colored folks cross the street rather than get in his way. Truth is, blacks in the city are scared of him."

"Is there…any truth that he might be in the Klan?"

At this, Tillie's eyes widened for a moment, but then she resumed her impassive mask. "I've heard rumors," she said quietly. "We all have. That's why we cut him a wide berth. What's the matter, he giving your daddy a hard time?"

"That's what Cecil let on. Why is that, do you think?"

"Honey, your daddy doesn't say much, keeps a lot inside him, but I believe that down deep he's a good man who doesn't hold himself above others. Part of it, I think, is because he was so poor when he was coming up. Then, of course, there was what happened over there in Ko-rea."

"What do you mean?"

The woman looked at her in wonder. "You don't know?"

"No. Would you tell me, please?"

Tillie sighed, suggesting she was angry at herself for letting this slip. "Okay, but don't tell him this came for me. Promise?"

"Cross my heart," she replied, sweeping her fingers across her chest.

"Well, a few years back an old army buddy of your daddy's came over with his wife for dinner, remember?"

"I think so. He was from Michigan or something."

"Wisconsin. Anyway, way up north. So, your momma, bein' the way she is, wanted to put on airs for this man and his wife, so she asked me if I could prepare the dinner that night. I said what the heck, it was extra pay, and as it happened to be near the holidays, I needed the money.

"So, this man and his wife came over, and they were nice as could be, but your daddy's buddy couldn't get over how somebody like him could have a colored maid."

"Because he couldn't afford it?"

"No, because of what happened in Ko-rea. See, your daddy's buddy liked to drink a little, and after a few cocktails he got a little loose with his talk. And I don't know if it was because I was there and this was for my benefit, but he told a story about how your daddy got all shot up in a battle and a Negro soldier saved his life, even though he died in the process."

Marnie was stunned. "Really? This really happened?"

"According to this man, it did. Of course, your father being the way he is, he did his best to shush him, but it made me see your daddy in a whole new light. Truth be told, I didn't care much for your momma, but I think your daddy's heart is in the right place, even if he's not one to show it. Joe Bob Sutter, on the other hand…" Her voice trailed off, signaling that this conversation was over. "C'mon, now, finish your grits," Tillie said. "They're gettin' cold."

Chapter Eight

In addition to the progressive style of their music, which had begun with the release of *Rubber Soul* and was destined to grow by leaps and bounds with their next, as of yet unnamed LP that was slated for an early August release, the Beatles were constantly breaking new ground in the ways pop music was being presented to the public. In the spring of 1966, the group was again at the forefront, putting forth two revolutionary products that would have wildly mixed results.

Although rock and roll performers and bands, including the Beatles, had lip-synched their way through taped teen shows and even performed in full-length movies, the concept of a music video was unheard of. Thus, it was that the Fab Four turned up at a London area estate named Chiswick House for the filming of two videos that would feature their current singles "Rain" and "Paperback Writer." In the estate's beautifully landscaped gardens and arched glass atrium they lip-synched their way through both numbers while dressed in mismatched "mod" outfits and sunglasses. Though the format of the videos was fairly straightforward, without any plot or acting on the part of the boys, the cinematography techniques of artistic cutaways and multiple angle shots were groundbreaking. These videos would later be shown, with much fanfare and critical acclaim, on British television, and the ever-supportive *Ed Sullivan Show* in the United States.

However, a second idea would bring the boys their first truly negative reaction.

For years, Capitol Records had issued different versions of Beatles LPs in Britain and America. The UK albums invariably contained more tracks, which were mostly released as singles in the States. It was only natural that, in an effort to generate more sales and squeeze in an American album between *Rubber Soul* and the upcoming summer issue, an LP entitled *Yesterday... and Today* was cobbled together from those accumulated 1965 to early 1966 singles.

An Australian photographer named Bob Whitaker was awarded the task of producing the album cover. Whitaker was himself considered an *Avant Garde* artist who dabbled in what was classified as "surrealistic" imagery. This appealed mightily to the Beatles, who had been pushing the envelope in their music and looking to shed their "good lads" image for something a bit more edgy. So, when Whitaker came up with the concept of picturing the Fab Four in medical lab coats and draped with dismembered baby dolls and bloody slabs of red meat, they were all in. The Beatles themselves thought it was all good fun.

Capitol Records did not. When the president of the corporation phoned Brian Epstein in London and suggested the cover photo be changed to something more mainstream, the Beatles, who by now were not used to their wishes being challenged by anyone, flatly refused. Thus, something like half a million copies of the album were printed and in the process of being circulated when those distributors who had been shipped advance copies let out an understandable collective cry that they just could not display this kind of content on their store shelves. The Beatles, grudgingly, had to agree to an alternate vanilla cover of them sitting around an empty steamer trunk, while those half-million "butcher" covers had to be unpacked and the original front sleeve pasted over with the newer version.

When faced with the prospect of public derision, the Beatles wisely took a look at the big picture and decided to give in on this near disaster. Little did they know, as the summer of 1966 neared, that some interviews they had done way back in January would have a more far-reaching effect on their perception by the public, as well as the success of their upcoming tour, and would put them on a collision course with a teenaged female fan in, of all places, Memphis, Tennessee.

Chapter Nine

Marnie knew she had made a mistake in accepting Charlotte's invitation to an April slumber party even before she'd hung up the phone. It wasn't the *location* that troubled her; she had been a guest at the Perkins house dozens of times, and although Charlotte's parents were really conservative and took their Baptist religion seriously, they were always pleasant and welcoming. Mrs. Perkins was an especially good cook, and Marnie was fond of her crispy fried chicken and sweet potato pie, although they couldn't touch a bite until they'd all held hands and prayed over the food. On Sundays Mr. Perkins was one of the deacons at the church Marnie and her father attended, and he didn't seem to ever crack a smile until Reverend Hollis had closed the service and the congregation milled around on the front lawn of the steepled, white clapboard church and visited with each other before returning home.

As the owner of the neighborhood supermarket, Mr. Perkins did okay for himself, though Marnie wondered how long it would be before modern stores like Winn-Dixie and Kroger's invaded his territory. But although Sam Perkins was always friendly to her, she sensed a disquieting undercurrent about the man that she couldn't quite put her finger on.

Marnie also felt that as Charlotte had grown into her teens she had taken after her parents in their desire to climb the social ladder. Five years ago, they had moved into a larger house with a backyard patio, and even had someone come in once a week to do the gardening. Mrs. Perkins was quite involved not only with the church but the Women's Club, and her husband was on the board of the Chamber of Commerce. Charlotte never went as far as to put on airs about her family's upward mobility, but Marnie could tell that being part of the "in crowd" was important to her in everything from the clothes she wore to the air conditioner and television her parents had installed in her room (they already had a large RCA console color TV in the living room). As far as her friendship with Marnie, it still seemed fairly strong and had weathered the ever-shifting alliances that junior high produced, but at times it felt like Marnie's friendship was one of the last threads of childhood that Charlotte still clung to. It was for this reason that Marnie felt she *had* to accept the slumber party invitation. What gave her pause for concern was who else had been invited.

Betty Lou Majors was a raven-haired beauty with a figure that was at least a couple years ahead of her age. She hardly socialized with the boys in their grade, opting to keep company with the older guys at Memphis Central High School, which the girls would be attending for tenth grade when they graduated from Hillcrest Junior High. Betty Lou was the touchy-feely sort who laughed too loud at jokes and sometimes played the dumb damsel in distress at school, usually to the teachers. That she would become a cheerleader at Central was a foregone conclusion, and Betty Lou made sure that when she entered a room, everyone there knew it.

As the unofficial "Miss Hillcrest Junior High," Betty Lou surrounded herself with like-minded girls who enjoyed basking in her reflected glory. They sat at their own eight-seat circular table in the lunchroom, and woe to those who would try to secure the table or fill in an empty seat if any one of the eight were absent. (Usually, coats or books were piled on those seats anyway, to discourage any attempt).

As for her family, the Majors were fairly well-to-do owners of the largest dry cleaners in the area (not that they lifted a finger in its daily operation, unlike Sam Perkins at his grocery store) who employed others—always white—to see after things. Betty Lou had two older brothers who were star athletes at Central, one in baseball, the other football, and who tooled around in a cherry red '62 Impala with a 409 engine that had all the girls drooling. Mr. Majors drove a Lincoln Continental.

The thing was that girls were always trying to worm their way into Betty Lou's sorority at Hillcrest, usually to be turned away with great embarrassment. But Charlotte, in her role as aspiring "popular girl," was not to be denied, hence her hopeful invitation to Betty Lou and a couple of her most trusted disciples for a Saturday night slumber party that was, to Charlotte's relief and happiness, accepted. And though Betty Lou had done a little tongue-clucking when Charlotte had answered her inquiry as to whom *else* had been invited, she had still agreed to attend.

Thus, it was that Marnie, her trusty sleeping bag

from camping trips rolled and slung over her shoulder, approached the Perkins residence after being dropped off by her father, who would be enjoying a rare night out playing cards at the home of one of the guys from the police department.

"It's gonna be great, and I'm gonna have a good time," she said to herself as she rang the doorbell. "Please, Lord, let me have a good time."

Mrs. Perkins answered the door, a welcoming smile plastered across her face. "Oh, hello, Marnie," she trilled, "you just caught us." Charlotte came up behind her mom, followed by Mr. Perkins, who was holding a tray of finger sandwiches, toothpick-skewered with a decorative stuffed olive and covered with Saran wrap. "Charlotte's dad and I are going a couple doors down for bridge with the Langfords," she explained. Then she turned to her daughter. "Charlotte, I left the Langfords' number by the phone in the kitchen. Give us a ring if you need us."

"Yes, Mom," said Charlotte dutifully, as if they'd been over this a couple hundred times already.

They sidestepped Marnie and scuttled out the front door as Charlotte blew out a sigh of relief. "Thank God we won't have them hovering over us all night," she said. "And knowing the Langfords, they won't be home till late." She made the motion of tipping a glass back to her lips, and Marnie nodded in understanding.

Scant seconds later, the other sleepover guests arrived, bounding out of Betty Lou's father's Lincoln. Falling in behind their leader were Amy Barnham and Peggy Steele, both of them untrustworthy weasels in Marnie's eyes. "I hope y'all are ready for a party," said Charlotte as she ushered the trio inside. "We've got the whole house to ourselves all night! My parents probably won't be home until after midnight."

"Cool!" said Peggy, a pasty-faced girl with a slight case of acne.

"Yeah, that's really boss, Char," agreed Amy, who was a couple ticks more attractive, but not much. Betty Lou definitely chose girls for her gang who couldn't compete in the looks department, though all three sported almost identical bouffants.

"My mom set up a ton of food for us," Charlotte gushed, trying too hard. "There's pigs in a blanket, potato chips, Cheese Doodles, Jiffy Pop, and two kinds of ice cream for dessert."

"Yum!" said Betty Lou, giving her approval. Amy and Peggy agreed.

"So, what do you want to do first?" asked Charlotte. "Watch some TV in the living room?"

"Nah, the Saturday night shows are dopey," said Betty Lou. "*Jackie Gleason* is for old fogeys, and *Flipper*, with whatever comes after it—"

"*Please Don't Eat the Daisies*—" blurted Marnie, who often watched both shows.

"—are for little kids," finished Betty Lou with a dismissive wave of her hand.

"So why don't we change into our PJs, take the food up to my room and listen to some records? I've got a ton."

"Sounds great!" said Amy.

They each carried a tray of snacks, along with some cold Cokes and Dr. Peppers, up to Charlotte's room, which was done in a kind of Pepto-Bismol pink with white trim, a white double bed, and white shag carpet. A window unit air conditioner hummed, though it was hardly a sticky Memphis evening; Marnie was sure this was just for show. There were stacks of *Tiger Beat* and *Seventeen* magazines placed randomly around the room to be flipped through.

"What records have you got?" asked Peggy, leafing through a dog-eared *Tiger Beat.*

"Well, there's the Righteous Brothers, the Association, the Stones, the Beach Boys, Tommy Roe…" She kept flipping album covers. "Paul Revere and the Raiders… and I've got all the Beatles albums, too."

Marnie was about to open her mouth reflexively when Betty Lou said, "I don't know, I'm kinda tired of them." This was obviously a dig at Marnie, whom everyone in the room knew was a Beatles fanatic. The other girls cut their eyes at Marnie, seeing if she'd take the bait.

Marnie did a mental "count to five" and said, "Um, why do you say that?"

"Well, for one thing," began Betty Lou, "I don't like their songs anymore. They used to be so much fun, like in *A Hard Day's Night.* How come they can't play fun stuff like that anymore? Why do they have to be so serious? And you can't dance to it, either. I went to a dance over at Central," she said in an obvious attempt to impress the others, "and the only Beatles songs they played were from a couple years ago. I think they're wearing out."

"I don't know, Betty Lou," replied Marnie, picking her words carefully as Charlotte looked on anxiously, slowly chewing her pig in a blanket, "I just think that they're, you know, getting a little older and all, and the words and stuff reflect that."

"Listen, Marnie," retorted Betty Lou, "when I hear a song on the radio, I'm not looking for a *message*… I just want a good tune I can dance to." Amy and Peggy nodded in agreement.

"I guess," said Marnie, giving in before Charlotte choked on her hot dog.

But Betty Lou smelled blood and wouldn't let it go. "I don't even think they're cute anymore," she pressed, "but maybe that's just me. Which one is *your* favorite, Marnie?" She popped a Cheese Doodle into her mouth and chased it with a swig of Dr. Pepper.

"I dunno," said Marnie as the Beach Boys' *Surfin' USA* album began to spin, courtesy of Charlotte. "In the beginning I was a real Paul fan; I mean, you've got to admit he's a cute guy." Amy and Peggy seemed about to nod in agreement but stopped themselves before they displeased their leader. "But since then, I've kinda become a John fan. There's just something about him."

"He's married, you know," spat Betty Lou.

"Yes, I'm aware of that."

"And you still think he's cute?"

"I don't see how that changes anything."

"Well, maybe *you* don't," said Betty Lou, who let her words hang in the air before abruptly switching gears. "Hey, why don't we do our nails?"

Charlotte, obviously relieved to be off the topic, said, "I'll get some nail polish remover. Who brought polish?" An examination of all the girls' overnight bags—except Marnie's, because she never wore it— revealed a handful of Maybelline polish bottles. "You can borrow some of mine," she whispered to Marnie as she moved toward her makeup dresser.

"Thanks."

For the next hour or so things went rather smoothly, and Betty Lou even deigned it acceptable to play the *Help!* album as they painted each other's fingernails and toenails and chatted about the latest gossip at Hillcrest Junior High. For a few fleeting minutes Marnie felt she'd weathered the storm and that it would be smooth sailing from there. But she had underestimated the depth of Betty Lou Majors' mean streak.

It started with the girl declaring, "I'm bored," sending Charlotte into a panic. But then, Betty Lou came up with a quick solution to her problem: "Hey, Char, want to raid your parents' liquor cabinet?"

"What?"

"You know, where they keep the booze. Let's have a few drinks, liven things up. They'll never know."

Charlotte blanched. "Gee whiz, Betty Lou, I don't know—"

"Oh, don't be such a baby, Charlotte," cut in Peggy. "Surely you've sneaked a drink before."

Marnie thought she knew the answer to this. Charlotte, much the same as herself, might've had an experimental sip (Roy had let her sample a drop of his Jack Daniels once, probably to discourage her from ever touching the stuff, and she'd quickly spit it out, bringing a smile to his face), but even at parties where a flask of whisky or some cans of beer had popped up, her friend was more likely to decline. However, she was now being tested, and Marnie saw it as a part of her initiation into the "popular girl" group.

"W-why sure I have, Peggy," she replied, pulling herself together. "It's just that I don't know what they have in there."

"Well, why don't we take a look, then?" prodded Amy.

"I guess so."

The quintet padded downstairs to the kitchen, where Charlotte pointed a somewhat shaky finger to a cabinet over the sink.

"Ah, hah!" said Betty Lou. "Strategically placed out of the reach of children." She snapped her finger a few times and ordered, "Step stool, please."

Charlotte dutifully produced one from the pantry closet, and Betty Lou climbed atop it. "Now what do we have here," she muttered, rummaging through the bottles. "Gotta find one that's already been cracked open, but nowhere near empty." She moved some of the bottles around, cried "Eureka!" and pulled out a somewhat dusty, almost full bottle of Bacardi rum. "Perfect," she declared. "Obviously not one of their favorites, 'cause it was way in the back. But it's been opened. Anyone for rum and Cokes?"

"Sounds great!" crowed Peggy.

"Then grab a few bottles of Coke and crack some ice cubes into a bowl, Amy. Char, can you find us some clean glasses?"

"Sure."

Marnie looked on with trepidation. This was surely going to happen. How would she play it? As if reading her mind, Betty Lou said, "You joining us, Marnie? We'll understand if you want out."

But the implication was clear. She was being challenged. "Count me in," she said.

They brought the fixings upstairs and pulled together the remainders of their snacks. Betty Lou, who'd obviously had some experience in mixology, filled each medium-sized jelly glass with ice, Coca-Cola, and a healthy slug of Bacardi. "Char, you got a spoon I can mix this with?" she said.

"Coming right up," she answered, and rose to leave the room, but not before she shot a dubious look at Marnie.

Once the drinks were stirred, Betty Lou lifted her glass. "To good friends," she intoned.

"Good friends," murmured Marnie as they clinked glasses.

This can't be so bad. Didn't I read somewhere that rum and Coke is a favorite Beatle drink? Maybe if I pretend I'm just having a drink with the boys—

Betty Lou's voice broke her reverie. "Marnie, what you waitin' on, girl?" All the others held forth empty glasses.

"Oops, sorry. Down the hatch," she said, and drained the dark liquid. It was sweet and fizzy, and the rum, instead of making her gag, went down smoothly and warmed her insides.

I think we'll have another," said Betty Lou.

And so it went. The more they drank, the more chips they ate, and the salty snacks led to more drinks. By 11 PM they were smashed. They had been chatting about their favorite and most detested Hillcrest teachers when Betty Lou suddenly blurted, "So, who's made out with the boy, here? And I don't just mean a peck on the cheek. You have to have French kissed. It's all in the tongue action."

They all giggled. Except Marnie. Now, she had, indeed, kissed a boy—Todd Frazier, whom she'd "gone out with" for a whopping three weeks back in February, but she'd hardly classify it as "making out."

Betty Lou, on the other hand, was all too eager to regale the other girls with her tales of romance with the older (tenth grade) boys at Central. Peggy and Amy followed suit with their stories, which of course paled in comparison; even Charlotte came up with a tale about a makeout session with the boy named Paul Matts, who was semi-popular at Hillcrest and therefore acceptable to Betty Lou.

Then she turned to Marnie. "So, what about you, Miss Priss? Too shy to kiss and tell? Or is it just that you got nothing *to* tell?"

Before she could even respond, Charlotte came to her defense and slurred, "She's got stories, don't you worry. C'mon, Marnie, fess up."

Marnie shot a dagger-filled look at her and said, "Listen, I'd just rather not."

Everyone fell silent. Then Betty Lou said, "Don't tell me it was that Jewboy, Myles Goldfarb."

Charlotte, after a sharp intake of breath, managed a shaky, "Now, Betty Lou—"

But Marnie wasn't going to let her friend fight her battles. "And what if it was?" she hissed, her eyes narrowing to slits.

"It's just that… that... I would think you'd have enough pride to keep away from members of that tribe," said Betty Lou airily.

"Really? And just what makes people of *that tribe* so horrible?" she shot back.

"They're just… different," was the answer. "And besides, everyone at school knows Myles is strange. Always with his nose in a book, reading about who knows what. And he never goes to parties—"

"Because he's never invited!" Marnie argued.

"And is it any wonder? C'mon, Marnie, you know he's weird, and probably a sissy, too. Fact is, you're probably the only girl—only *kid* at Hillcrest that hangs out with him. Even Charlotte doesn't like him. Isn't that right, Char?"

The stunned girl managed a "Um…well…"

"Don't bring her into this," said Marnie, her tone a bit more threatening.

"And what about his *parents?*" said Betty Lou, ratcheting up the venom. "I've got it on good authority that his mother has been seen staggering out of some honky-tonks on Beale Street, sometimes in the *afternoon*, and that his big executive daddy has had to go down there and pull her out of others."

"That's a lie."

"Says you. Maybe your own daddy has had to go roust her for creatin' a disturbance or public drunkenness. You ever ask him?"

Marnie stared at her, the blood pounding in her ears.

"'Course, it could be worse, Marnie. I mean, it's not like you're goin' around kissin' Nigras—" Her pronunciation of the last word was so close to something else, a word that made her think of Tillie, and Birmingham, and Greensboro, and so much else that had become abhorrent to Marnie that she couldn't hold back anymore. It was time to give Betty Lou Majors what-for.

Marnie Culpeper stood up wobbily and pointed a newly polished fingernail down at her tormentor, who sat Indian-style like the others, gaping upwards. "Now y'all listen to *me*, Betty Lou," she began. "It's one thing to come over here and lord it over everybody about how cool and popular and whatever that you think you are. Maybe it makes you feel important, like when you're at school. And maybe the fact that your dopey friends here *yes* you to death 'cause they're afraid you'll turn on 'em, gives you the courage to feel like you can get away with sayin' hurtful, *hateful* crap to nobodies like me.

"But you hear me now, Betty Lou Majors. People like Myles Goldfarb are worth a *hunnerd* of your friends, and someday you're gonna regret runnin' down people of his race and colored folks and everybody else your tiny brain has been taught to hate. And as far as bringing my daddy into this, you…you…" She stopped herself, trying to keep the room from tilting, but it was no use. The combination of the alcohol, rising to her feet, and her boiling anger had created a toxic mix, and Marnie Culpeper simply could not help it when she discharged a geyser of rum/Coke/Cheese Doodles/potato chips/pigs in a blanket all over Charlotte's white shag rug, as well as Betty Lou Majors's upturned face and impeccably coiffed bouffant.

"Ewww! Ewww! Ewww!" screamed Betty Lou, who had belatedly brought her hands up to shield her eyes. Marnie just stood there, gently swaying, surprised at what she had wrought, as Charlotte, Amy, and Peggy dragged the still-screaming girl to the hallway bathroom and started running the faucet. Marnie couldn't decide whether she felt better because she'd sicked up the alcohol, or because she'd nailed Betty Lou right between the eyes. Then she staggered over to Charlotte's bed and passed out on the quilt patterned with teddy bears.

* * *

Marnie came to what seemed like hours later, sledgehammers whacking the inside of her head. She lay on her friend's bed, a pillow under her twisted tresses and a cool towel compress across her forehead, held in place by Charlotte, who sat on a chair she'd pulled up to the bed. The room smelled nauseatingly of Lysol.

"Wh-what time is it?" Marnie croaked, her mouth dry and foul-tasting.

"Around twelve-thirty," Charlotte answered.

"Where are the others?"

Charlotte sighed. "They went home, Marnie. Soon as we got Betty Lou cleaned up she called her pa and he came and carted them off." She shook her head. "Girl, how much did you *eat?*" she marveled.

"I'm so embarrassed," Marnie said with a moan. "Did I really puke all over her?"

"Uh-huh," said her friend. "It was pretty gross. I cleaned the rug, though. It came out okay."

"Where are your folks?"

"Oh, I should think they'll be home any minute."

"What are you gonna tell them?"

"Well, I put the rum bottle back in the closet, and hopefully they'll never go looking for it 'cause it's like three quarters empty. I'll just tell them Betty Lou had a bad reaction to the hot dogs or something,and the other girls left because she was their ride."

"Do you want *me* to go?"

Charlotte sighed again. "Nah, that's okay, Marnie." She squeezed her friend's hand. "But we should try to get an Alka-Seltzer or some Pepto-Bismol into you so you're not a disaster tomorrow morning."

"Good, because to tell you the truth, the room is still spinning a little bit."

"I can imagine."

Marnie laid the back of her free hand over the towel compress and began to cry. "I'm so sorry, Char," she sobbed. "I ruined this whole night for you. Good Lord, I can just imagine what Betty Lou's gonna put out around school on Monday—"

"Hey," Charlotte soothed, "don't you worry your pretty head about all that. Truth be told, from the way she and her friends acted tonight, and the spiteful things she said, I don't know as I'd ever want to hang out with her, or her crew. And, tell you what, the look on her face when the puke hit her was kinda unforgettable." She reached over and wiped away the tears from under Marnie's eyes.

"But I have to tell you something, Marnie," she continued, "and it might be hard for you to understand. Maybe I'm only saying this 'cause I'm still a little drunk, but you gotta tone it down if you want us to stay best friends. You just can't go around defending the downtrodden of the world, for whatever reasons you do it. I can take all the Beatles stuff 'cause, well, it's all harmless, but when you get onto some other topics—"

"Like Myles, for instance?"

"Like Myles, and the coloreds, and Vietnam, and whatever-all has you worried on a particular day that makes it pure-d uncomfortable to be around you. What I'm saying is, I want to be your friend, Marnie, but you're not makin' it easy."

"I'm sorry, Char, I'll try harder," she earnestly whispered. "Now, you want to go grab that Pepto-Bismol?"

Chapter Ten

Even before the Beatles departed from London in early June for the European leg of their summer tour, a three-date stay in Germany, they were starting to be asked questions about the hot button issues of the world. One constant topic was the segregationist policies that were rampant in the southern United States. The other was the troubling war in Vietnam.

By the beginning of 1966 the United States had nearly 200,000 troops on the ground where, combined with over 500,000 South Vietnamese soldiers, they tried to fend off the advance of the communist North Vietnamese forces in an attempt to preserve democracy in what was considered a vital corner of Southeast Asia.

US involvement in Vietnam actually had begun in the 1950s during the presidency of World War II hero Dwight D. Eisenhower, who had come to the aid of his wartime ally France, which ruled Vietnam as a colony but were in danger of being overthrown. When communist North Vietnamese forces, bolstered by China and Russia, effectively ousted the French, the United States persisted in the effort to stem the tide of communism, as they had in the Korean War. John F. Kennedy had continued America's involvement to help the South Vietnamese, and after his assassination, Lyndon Johnson had somewhat stepped up the initiative to try to bring the conflict to an end or force some kind of settlement like the one reached in Korea, which had partitioned that country into communist and democratic halves.

But it seemed that as the months dragged on, casualties were mounting, and the advent of live, in-color TV coverage was making Americans and people all over the world—including the four young men from Liverpool—uneasy. Despite the pleas of Brian Epstein to steer clear of any controversial statements on world issues like Vietnam, John Lennon commented, "I don't like what's happening there."

His bandmate Paul McCartney offered, "If you can say (as an entertainer) that war is no good, and a few people believe you, then it might be good. I can't say too much, though. That's the trouble."

And though these comments were hardly radical in nature, and never went near the communism vs. democracy debate, the Beatles' somewhat negative take on the war being waged in Southeast Asia seemed to put them on the side of liberal factions opposed to the war. Questions about the conflict would thus dog them throughout the upcoming tour.

When the Beatles' entourage landed in Munich, it was their first visit to the still-divided Germany since 1963. The plan was for the group to perform not in outdoor sports arenas but more manageable indoor venues. Even so, this was quite a jump from their earliest German concerts. As teens the Beatles, at first with Pete Best as their drummer, had ventured to Hamburg with the lure of paid gigs where they could both enjoy the benefits of living without parental supervision while honing their talents as a performing band. And perform they did, night after night, for hours on end, at seedy clubs with names like the Kaiserkeller and the Indra, sometimes popping amphetamines to keep their energy level going, while living in squalid accommodations like a back room behind the movie screen in a dingy theater. They had returned to England broke and exhausted, but sporting a new hairdo bestowed upon them by a female artist friend and becoming tighter as a group, though virtually all of their repertoire at the time were covers of American hits.

When they took the stage (following a series of warm-up acts, which had come to be their custom) at the 3,500 seat Circuskrone for the two Munich shows, they did so as polished rock and roll royalty, attired not in the leather jackets and pants they'd worn in 1962, nor the dark Edwardian suits and ties of 1963-1964, but bottle green outfits with silk lapels and high collared lime and yellow shirts.

The performances they gave could hardly be termed as great, even when compared to their last British concert in May, but it hardly mattered to a fan base starved for a look at their long-lost rockers. A wall of sound so incredible that it overwhelmed any attempt of the group to stay in tune or even remember their songs' lyrics would begin with the opening chord of each number and continue for its duration.

But while the adulation for the band was extraordinary, there seemed now to be an edge—a frightening edge—that had not been as discernible in previous years. For one thing, the police who provided security for the concerts were overly aggressive towards the young fans, grabbing and even beating those who tried to get closer to the stage. The Beatles, who blew through what by now had become a standard set of eleven songs, mostly oldies mixed with current singles like "We Can Work It Out" and "Paperback Writer," were relieved to exit the stage before they themselves were physically assaulted.

From Munich, it was on to Essen via a chartered train usually reserved for use by heads of state. After the obligatory press conference in which they were asked the usual banal questions, including what they thought of those questions ("They're a bit stupid," said Lennon honestly, to some applause.), they took the stage in an even more riotous concert hall, where the security personnel wore trench coats and employed tear gas and guard dogs to keep the crowd in check.

Hamburg, the last stop in Germany, gave the Beatles an opportunity to connect with old friends they'd made in the early 60s. But the ritual of sitting through the press conferences was grating on them, with one reporter even asking Lennon why the boys had become "so horrid and snobby." On June 26, they played two shows at the 5,600 seat Ernst-Merck Halle, which were unremarkable but thankfully less threatening in tone.

As it would turn out, the German dates were only a harbinger of what was to come.

Chapter Eleven

It was a typical Friday afternoon in mid-May when Tillie answered the phone as she was beginning to prepare dinner for Roy and his daughter. Marnie, who was sitting at the kitchen table doing some homework, barely took notice as the housekeeper said, "Culpeper residence," followed by a series of "uh-huhs," "yes sirs," and finally, "I'll make sure to tell her." Then she hung up the phone and started putting back the dinner fixings into the refrigerator.

"What's the matter, Tillie?" asked the girl.

"Looks like my work is done here, honey," she answered. "It appears you got a date this evening."

"With who?"

"With your daddy. He wants you to get cleaned up and put on a nice dress. Seems like he's taking you out for a bite to eat."

Marnie was taken back. It had been quite a while since she'd had a night out with her father, and she was instantly excited. Perhaps it signaled he was emerging from the funk he'd been in the past few months. She even dared to wonder if he had good news to announce, such as the long-awaited promotion to lieutenant he'd been after. She packed up her school stuff and scurried upstairs, already picking out the dress she'd be wearing that evening, the pink one with small yellow daisies that he liked so much.

* * *

By the time Roy got home from work, Tillie had been gone for an hour. He pulled into the driveway in his immaculate 1960 Ford Fairlane, a powder blue sedan with horizontal rear fins and whitewall tires that he washed and waxed once a month and always garaged. His rather beat-up pickup truck was relegated to a spot next to the one-car garage, where it awaited his next hunting trip.

"You ready, sweet pea?" he called upstairs.

"Just a second!" Marnie called back while applying some conservative lipstick. She bounded down the stairs, her hair swaying from side to side, and greeted him with a big hug. Her father had dressed in his "going out" ensemble of a button down short-sleeved shirt, Haggar slacks and loafers. She inhaled the scent of his Old Spice aftershave.

"Now don't you look the picture," he said, holding her out at arm's length. "And you wore my favorite sundress."

"Of course," she replied, batting her eyes coquettishly. "Wouldn't want to embarrass you out in public."

"Never. So, what's your choice?" Roy knew that whenever they went out to eat, which was rare, it came down to their mutual favorites in the Beale Street area: Charlie Vergos' Rendezvous for mouthwatering ribs, or Dyer's Burgers.

"Dyer's."

"Sounds good. Let's get after it, then. I hardly ate lunch and I'm starving."

She slid into the front bench seat of the Fairlane, redolent with the cardboard pine tree car freshener that hung from the rear-view mirror, as Roy started the car and gunned the finely-tuned motor. In fact, her father was proud that he did just about all the maintenance on the Fairlane, whose latest paste waxing now shone in the gloaming of the evening.

As they backed out of the narrow driveway that led from the garage, Marnie reflexively reached for the AM radio and clicked it on. It was tuned to a local affiliate of CBS where a war correspondent was announcing the latest casualty report in Vietnam.

"No," said Roy quietly as Marnie swiftly punched in WHBQ for some rock and roll. Not surprisingly, the Beatles' "Day Tripper" was playing, but Marnie could sense her dad cutting her a sideways look. So, with a dramatic sigh she switched to a country station, where Eddie Arnold was singing "I Want to Go with You."

"Well, that's appropriate, seeing how we're going on this fancy date," she commented.

"Uh-huh," he said with a faint smile.

The destination for this evening, Dyer's Burgers, was located on Beale Street, which had come to be known as the hub of Memphis blues music in the early 1900s. Unfortunately, by 1966 the famous thoroughfare had fallen upon hard times fueled by segregation issues, and many businesses had closed, while others seemed a bit seedy. Dyer's was one of the few family businesses to keep its doors open and had been a personal favorite of Roy and his fellow officers since he had joined the force.

They coasted to a stop at the curb right in front of the humble restaurant and entered, greeted by the owner, Mr. Aaron, who was always happy to see The Sarge or any of his comrades. "My, my, this little lady's gettin' bigger every day," he said, "and isn't she purty." He steered them towards a table in the half-full eatery.

Roy and Marnie ordered their usual meal, called the "Double Double," which consisted of two thin beef patties that were not grilled or seared on a flat top skillet, but fried in a vat of aged grease, topped with cheese, and served on a soft bun with onions, pickles and mustard—but no ketchup. A side order of French fries rounded out the calorie-packed plate. Both also ordered sweet teas and awaited their feast, a pungent bouquet of meat and grease wafting from the kitchen area.

"So, are you gettin' anxious for the end of school?" asked Roy to get things started.

"You bet," Marnie replied as two large Coke glasses with flared tops arrived, filled with ice and amber tea and complemented by a plastic straw and lemon wedge.

"How do you see your grades turnin' out?" he asked, taking a sip.

"Well, about the same as usual, even though we still have to take finals. Maybe a B in math; and then, I hope, mostly As."

"Good deal. I'm proud of you, Marnie, pullin' good marks without my help, because you know I'm lost on a lot of this stuff."

"Well, you're just good at other things, Daddy. It's just not school-type stuff."

"Yeah? Like what?"

"Like hunting, for example. You can track a deer like an Indian, and you know how to find all the good fishing holes while everybody else is getting skunked."

He gave a modest shrug and said, "That ain't no big deal."

"Oh yeah? And how many men nowadays can fully tune a car? And fix just about anything around the house?"

"Yeah, well—"

"And one more thing. How many men have what it takes to lead a squad of police out there on the streets of a big city like Memphis, where it can be really dangerous?"

"Darlin'," he said quietly, "I'm just a sergeant, not the guy in charge."

"Please, Daddy. You're not gonna actually tell me that Lt. Sutter really runs things. It's *you* the men listen to."

"Easy, now. He's still my boss. We might not always see eye to eye, but his rank commands respect. One thing I learned in the army was to respect the chain of command."

"Even if he's a racist?"

Roy's eyes widened at the sound of the word. "Now hush," he whispered. "There'll be no talk like that, especially in public like we are."

"Okay, but you know I'm right," she hissed, defiantly tilting her chin upwards.

"He's just…more old-fashioned," said Roy.

"Yeah, well, in case he hasn't noticed, the times are changing 'round here," said Marnie, "and it's something that can't be stopped. Why, just a couple years ago people like Tillie couldn't even use a white restroom or take their clothes to a white laundry. And then, you've got the Klan—"

"Sshh."

"I know they're around here, Daddy, everyone does, and that they still have big old get-togethers out in the woods past the city limits."

"That's none of your concern, Marnie."

"Isn't it? When my father is meant to protect and serve the citizens of this town—*all* the citizens of this town—and I still hear tell of Negroes disappearing, getting lynched or beaten up, or having crosses burned on their property?"

Roy blew out a large breath.

"What is it?"

He looked at her and smiled. "You're just growing up so fast, darlin', and sometimes I think you've got the weight of the world on your pretty little shoulders. Why can't you just enjoy being a kid? You'll have the rest of your life to deal with adult problems, and I guarantee you, they'll be rollin' up on you before you know it."

Mercifully for Roy, the burgers arrived, hot and greasy and delicious. Father and daughter dug in, and for a few minutes nothing could be heard but the casual conversation from other tables of the quickly filling restaurant.

Marnie was popping the last of her fries into her mouth when Roy pushed away his plate and said, "Okay, so now I got to talk to you about something serious."

"Oh… kay," she said slowly. "Something happened at work?"

"Well, kinda. Marnie, the other day I got a call from Betty Lou Majors' momma."

Marnie could feel her Double Double fall to the bottom of her stomach. "She called you at *work?*"

"That she did." He signaled their waiter, a teenaged girl not much older than his daughter, for another sweet tea. Marnie declined hers. "Now," he said gently, "do y'all want to tell me your version of what happened over at the Perkins' house when you had the sleepover?"

"What'd Mrs. Majors tell you?"

"I want to hear your side, because believe me, I got an earful from her. So, go on."

"Well, okay," she began, "but you're not gonna be happy when I'm done."

"Just get it out, darlin', and then I'll decide if I'm happy."

Marnie looked at her father, with his blocky, crewcut head that sat atop broad shoulders, his eyes fixing her with a steely glare, and figured he must be especially effective in prying confessions out of criminals. She also figured there was no sense in trying to lie her way out of it, so she told him everything, with as much detail as she could remember. Rivulets of sweat snaked down her back by the time she reached the end. Halfway through she had begun to tear up, and Roy had deftly plucked a paper napkin from the red metal table dispenser and slid it across so she wouldn't have to pause. "So that's it," she finally said. "As far as I can remember."

"So, you're sayin' it was Betty Lou's idea to do the drinking."

"Yessir. Why, what did her mother say?"

"I don't think you have to guess too hard on that." He was still stone-faced. "So, what you're telling me is, she started runnin' down your friend Myles's mom—"

"And Jews and Negroes in general—"

"Okay, okay," he said placing his palms in the air to stop her.

"No, it's *not* okay, Daddy. And then, when she brought *you* into it, I just snapped. I know it was the liquor talking, but I just wasn't gonna let her get away with that."

"And you really threw up all over her?"

"Well, yeah."

"Good Lord." He shook his head, and Marnie thought she detected the faintest of smiles, although it could have been hopeful imagination at work. "And Charlotte's parents never found out about this?"

"Not unless Mrs. Majors called them, too."

"Doesn't look like she did. Well, anyway, Betty Lou gave her mom a completely different story, picked you out as the ringleader, said you got really aggressive the more you drank."

"I figured."

"But that doesn't make what you did right. I haven't raised my little girl to be some falling-down drunk, even if it is on a dare. I wish you could've found a way out of it."

"I couldn't. I know it was wrong to join them, but I couldn't."

"And what if someone dares you to do something else, like these drugs I been hearing about?"

"I'd like to think I've learned my lesson. Lord, Daddy, if I even *smell* rum again I think I'll puke."

Finally, he allowed himself a thin smile. "Well, then, I told Mrs. Majors I'd talk to you and get to the bottom of it, and I did. And to make *sure* you learned your lesson, I'm gonna let you think about it for the next two weeks 'cause you're grounded. And during that time, just to make sure you're not bored, I want you to scrape down the garage 'cause it's due for a painting. It ain't too big, and I got me a good scraper you can use. That should keep you busy till the end of school."

"Okay."

Roy drained the rest of his second sweet tea and pushed it away. He said, "Baby girl, you've got a good heart, always have. But I want you to study on some things while you're scraping away.

"Personally, I don't care for anybody in the Majors family. The two boys are troublemakers who've had brushes with the law, and I expect that Betty Lou is another bad apple. But her daddy is on the building commission in the city and he has a lot of pull. Me, I'm just a lowly civil servant, but I don't trust him. There's a lot of people in this town who I don't necessarily like, Marnie, like the guy we were talking about earlier. But one thing that life has taught me is that sometimes to get along, you have to go along. I might not agree with people like Lt. Sutter and Betty Lou's daddy, but I know they have power that I don't. So, I've got to watch it, and so do you. Marnie, you just can't go around spoutin' off when you feel that you, or someone you know, has been put upon. That includes people like Myles and Tillie and whoever else you think is gettin' the short end of the stick. You'll just end up making things harder on yourself, and I can't always be there to pull your fat out of the fire. You follow me?"

"Yes, Daddy," she said. "Can I tell you something?"

"Yes, what?"

"You've got a good heart, too."

"Thanks," he said gently. "Now let's get out of here. Can you manage an ice cream cone? Long as you don't let it drip on the car seat, that is."

"I think so."

Roy paid the bill and they left Dyer's Burgers, hand-in-hand.

Chapter Twelve

The Beatles again took to the skies on June 27, departing for a grueling sixteen-hour flight to Tokyo. Unfortunately, what was to be a brief refueling stopover in Anchorage, Alaska, turned into an overnight stay due to Japan being pummeled by Typhoon Kit, packing winds of 195 MPH. As a result, Brian Epstein checked them into the top floor suite of the local Anchorage Hotel. Of course, when word got out that the Beatles were actually in Anchorage, hordes of Alaskan teens camped under their hotel window, singing and pleading for them to show themselves until a swiftly imposed 10 PM curfew cleared the streets. Early the next morning, they took off again for Japan.

The Fab Four emerged from the plane at Tokyo's Haneda Airport in traditional Japanese "happi" silk jackets, were bundled into a waiting vehicle, and took off for their hotel, escorted by a dozen police cars with sirens wailing. Apparently, government officials were concerned over threats from a right wing nationalist group that the Beatles—*Westerners*—were being allowed to perform at the Budokan, a martial arts arena that was used exclusively for events promoting Japanese culture and tradition.

Japan was still rebuilding, both economically and

emotionally, from their crushing defeat in World War II, which had culminated with the dropping of atomic bombs on the major cities of Hiroshima and Nagasaki. Traditionalists clinging pridefully to the old ways decried the intrusion of a British pop group, predicting that influences such as the Beatles on their impressionable youth would promote juvenile delinquency. Even the Prime Minister of Japan made clear his opposition to the visit.

From the other side came the argument that these four young men had been decorated by the Queen of the United Kingdom, and that their acceptance by the Japanese would not only strengthen their ties with the West going forward but would establish Japan as a country looking towards the future instead of dwelling upon its past. Thus, even though the Beatles seemed to exhibit characteristics valued by the Japanese such as good business sense, their individualism and emergence as anti-establishment spokesmen caused a divide that had the Japanese media in a tizzy.

As far as their Japanese fans were concerned, the Beatles had as yet not seen any, because security at the airport had kept them away. The four musicians found themselves sequestered in the presidential suite of the Hilton Hotel, with armed guards stationed outside the door and at every possible entry point to the hotel. They were under no circumstances allowed to leave their lodgings for the duration of their stay, except to perform at the Budokan. The only positives in this incarceration were that the boys were given the opportunity to relax a bit; most notably by collaborating on a large painting which would be auctioned for charity, an experience they quite enjoyed, and they were finally able to agree on a name for the new LP scheduled for its early August release: *Revolver*.

Of course, an introductory press conference had to be held at the hotel, and this one was packed with both Japanese and foreign media. Once again, the Beatles were peppered with mundane, if not ridiculous, questions about how they slept and how often they groomed their hair, their reaction to Queen Elizabeth and receiving medals from her, and what they thought about the Japanese fans they had yet to see.

But then, the questions turned more serious. John Lennon, who seemed bored and distant, proclaimed that they were against the use of nuclear armaments, which his bandmate McCartney quickly echoed. They also voiced their concern that the behavior of police and other security forces at their concerts was becoming too aggressive, and that the actions of their concert fans were no different than the exuberance displayed by crowds at football (soccer) matches all over the world, and much less physical in nature.

Finally, the subject turned to the war in Vietnam, which Epstein had specifically implored the boys to stay away from while in Asia. But the bandmates, especially Lennon and Harrison, had made it clear that going forward the Beatles would answer questions on this topic honestly. So, when a reporter asked Lennon for his opinion on the conflict, he replied, "Well, we think about it every day, and we don't agree with it and we think it's wrong."

The Budokan concerts were somewhat anti-climactic, more of a military maneuver than a celebration of music. Almost 8,400 law enforcement agents from plainclothes officers to snipers had been charged with ensuring the Beatles' safety before, during, and after the concerts. Their movements were planned to the minute, with the boys being whisked downstairs and through the Hilton's back entrance to bulletproof vehicles. Though it was rush hour, the roads had been cleared, and they motored to the arena past penned-in groups of fans, under bridges patrolled by riflemen. Also visible were right wing protesters in black and white trucks playing martial music over loudspeakers and flying banners telling the Beatles to go home. It was unlike anything Japan—or the Beatles—had ever experienced.

The concerts themselves had a strange feel as well, but for different reasons. The Beatles had become used to a wall of sound crashing down upon them for the length of their now-standard eleven song set, but when they took to the Budokan stage in their new mod matching suits, the crowds seemed eerily subdued. And it was no wonder—the powers that be had issued warnings that anyone standing, dancing, or even leaving their seats would be physically ejected from the arena. For the first time in a long time, the Beatles could actually hear themselves play. Unfortunately, their harmonies at times sounded flat, and they made many mistakes in the more intricate instrumental parts of the songs. Though it seemed that nobody cared, there were some rumblings that the abbreviated set was not worth the then-exorbitant amount of $24 for all but the cheapest seats. Still, the band agreed that their playing was off, and vowed to improve in future concerts.

Overall, the Beatles' Japanese tour dates were deemed a success because they had made a great deal of money. They had also opened the door to stronger cultural ties with the East, and they had avoided being killed, kidnapped, or otherwise harmed. The group left the land of the Rising Sun—whose culture had *not* been destroyed by their visit—relieved it was over, and somewhat positive that the climate of the tour could not help but improve on their next stop in the Philippines.

Chapter Thirteen

No matter what Marnie had going on any given Saturday, Beatles cartoons were a part of the itinerary. On this day after the school year ended, she had brought her washed laundry downstairs to the living room to do the folding while she tuned in. Out back she could hear her father doing his final prep work on the garage she had painstakingly scraped the past two weeks so he could apply a first coat of paint.

Beatles cartoons were now in their second year on ABC. Each episode bore the name of a Beatles song, with a somewhat flimsy plot constructed around it. That song would be played in its entirety somewhere in the plot sequence. In addition, there were sing-along features of other Beatle tunes with the full lyrics provided. Of course, Marnie always sang along, and she didn't need the lyrics.

As for the portrayal of her heroes, Marnie considered it a bit simplistic, from the herky-jerky animation to the somewhat stereotypical personas of the boys. John was portrayed as the wisecracking, jut-jawed leader; Paul was the exceedingly cute, stylish second-in-command; George was the secondary band member with a weird accent that didn't sound like any of the other guys; and Ringo was the big-nosed, clownish buffoon who was always giggling and whose Liverpudlian accent was way overdone. Of course, the Beatles were pictured as the lovable mop tops of *A Hard Day's Night* vintage.

There were usually two stories per half hour program, separated by commercials for Cap'n Crunch cereal, Mars candies like Three Musketeers and M&Ms (which promised to "melt in your mouth, not in your hand") and children's toys.

The first segment of today's show, "Eight Days a Week," involved a great movie actor named Lips Lovelace, who had lost his ability to kiss. So, he enlisted Paul to take his place, which of course led to Lovelace's female costar falling in love with the doe-eyed Beatle.

A commercial for Milky Way candy bars was on when the phone rang, so Marnie hoisted herself up from the living room floor and answered it.

"What's goin' on, Marnie? Enjoying your first day of vacation?" asked Myles sweetly.

"Oh yeah, for sure. Just folding some laundry that Tillie did."

"And watching Beatles cartoons, I'd assume?"

"You know me too well."

The boy laughed. "I was just wondering if maybe you'd want to knock a tennis ball around later on, or maybe tomorrow after you're done with church?"

"Sorry, can't," she answered. "I've gotta help Daddy around the house here today, but…" She paused.

"You still there?"

"Yeah, sorry. Listen, I've got an idea, Myles. Tomorrow afternoon after services is our church's big

Memorial Day weekend picnic. Would you like to come as my guest?"

"*Me?*"

"Yes, you. Why, what's the big deal?"

"Well, for one thing, I'm not a member of your congregation."

"So what? Other people bring a guest. Why can't I?"

"Well, what about your dad? I'm not sure if I'm totally welcome around him."

"I think you've got my father all wrong, Myles," she answered. "I bet he'd say yes. Besides, I'll really need someone to hang around with. Charlotte will be all tied up with that Tommy Plummer—"

"The jock guy?"

"One and the same. I think they're close to going out. And then, Betty Lou Majors and her buddies will be there and you *know* I don't want any part of them. And there will be a lot of great barbecue and field games and stuff for us to do. What do you say?"

"I say you'd better check this out with The Sarge first, and then give me a call if it's okay."

"All right, I'll do just that," she replied confidently.

By the time Roy trudged inside, sweaty from painting in the still-mild May climate, Marnie's confidence had waned a bit, but she had a secret weapon. "Get cleaned up a bit and sit down, Daddy," she sang, "I have a special lunch for you!"

"Do you really?" he said, arching an eyebrow.

"Uh-huh."

He took off his work boots, laid them on the stoop outside the side door, and washed his hands and face in the bathroom. "Little girl," he said, "you did a first-class job scraping the garage, even the part where you had to get on the ladder to reach. I've already got a first coat on the door, and the rest this afternoon should be a breeze."

"Want me to help?"

"Nope, you've done your share. So, what's this special lunch you're talkin' about?"

"Well, it's a sandwich Tillie makes me sometimes. She got it on good notice from a friend of hers who works up at Graceland—"

"Elvis's place?"

"Uh-huh. Well, supposedly Elvis's favorite all-time sandwich is…this one!" She removed a domed aluminum pot-top from the plate in front of him to reveal a still-warm, savory scented sandwich.

"What on earth do we have here?" he marveled.

"Here's how you make it," she explained proudly. "You put some butter in a pan and melt it, like you're making a grilled cheese. Then you slather two pieces of bread with peanut butter, slice up a ripe banana, get a couple strips of crispy bacon, and lay all that stuff inside the bread. Then you fry it up like a grilled cheese and voilà!"

Roy leaned sideways, observing the still-oozing sandwich from a few different angles. "And you say it's The King's favorite, huh?"

"That's the word. And here's a big ol' glass of milk to go with it, with ice cubes, just like you like it."

Roy took a preliminary bite, chewed a little, and smiled. "This is top-notch, baby girl," he said. "I'm glad you're learning from Tillie. If you become half the cook she is, you're gonna make some guy awful happy." He took a larger bite. "Now tell me what you want," he added, somewhat hampered by the gobs of peanut butter stuck to the roof of his mouth.

"What do you mean?"

"You've got that face on, honey. Like you need to ask me for something. So, let's have it."

She sighed. Nothing got past The Sarge. "Okay," she said. "Fact is, I'd like to invite my friend Myles to the picnic tomorrow."

He stopped chewing. "Myles *Goldfarb?*"

"How many Myleses do you think I know, Daddy? Of course, Myles Goldfarb."

"Gee, I don't know," he said, chewing more slowly. "Won't he feel out of place?"

"Not unless people make him feel that way."

"Gee, I don't know," he said again.

"Look at it this way, Daddy," she pressed, "Charlotte's got a new boyfriend, so I'd be a fifth wheel there, and I'm *sure* you don't want me going near Betty Lou and her bunch—"

"Okay, okay, I catch your drift," he said, taking a sip of iced milk. "Now, he isn't gonna show up wearing one of those Yamahas, is he?"

She laughed. "What?"

"You know, those beanie things the Jews wear."

"You mean a *yarmulke*. A Yamaha is a motorcycle, Daddy."

"Well, whatever."

"No, I don't think he'll wear one. Myles isn't super religious, anyway," she said, her eyes hopeful.

"Then I guess it's all right. Have his folks drop him here around noon, and he can ride over with us. But he can't be late. I'm helping with the cooking, and they're counting on me. As it is, I have to get over to the church grounds way early in the morning and get the barbecue smokers going."

"He won't be late, I promise." She hugged him around the neck from behind and kissed the top of his crew cut. "Thanks, Daddy."

"Sure," he said. "Now let me finish my lunch before it gets cold. I've got painting to do. Tell you one thing, though. I hope Elvis isn't making a habit of these sandwiches, or he's gonna turn into a blimp."

* * *

The First Baptist Church was one of Memphis's oldest white congregations, dating back to the early 1800s. Its membership had grown steadily over the years, and events such as today's summer kickoff picnic dotted its busy social calendar. It was also probably Roy's favorite day, as he was given a chance to do something he loved: prepare barbecue. As a child he had raptly watched his father smoke meats on a cooker fashioned from an old metal barrel cut in half. Hickory sticks would be fed into the bottom of the smoker until the desired temperature of around 275° was reached. Then, the cuts of meat, including pork butts and shoulder, ribs, and chickens split in half would be slowly roasted for hours, occasionally basted with a homemade sauce and turned. Other game meats such as venison and wild turkey often made the menu as well. Nothing went to waste in the Culpeper home.

The church had acquired three huge smokers that were used for outdoor gatherings such as today, and the fire was started by volunteers, including Roy, in the wee hours of the morning. Then, he and a couple other men would return around 8 AM and load the meats, which had been covered with a dry rub of salt, pepper, paprika, cayenne and brown sugar, into the smoker before returning home to clean up for services at 10 AM. With the church windows open to allow fresh air into the building warmed by the early summer heat, it was not unusual to see members of the congregation sniffing excitedly as barbecue smoke wafted its way inside. On one occasion, Reverend Hollis, a serious, stoic pastor on the best of days, even stopped his sermon midsentence to proclaim, "My goodness, can you smell that?"

After church, everyone would scurry home to change into more casual attire and reconvene on the vast mowed field behind the church where a number of long picnic tables and beverage stations had been set up, along with piles of paper plates, cups, and plastic cutlery. A variety of outdoor games had been planned for both adults and children, and a temporary stage had been erected for a three-piece country band featuring a banjo, guitar and fiddle.

Roy was just coming downstairs in his picnic attire of jeans, golf shirt and sneakers when the doorbell rang, signaling the arrival of Marnie's guest. "Oh, hello, Myles," Roy said, offering his beefy hand for a shake. "Come on in, she'll be right down."

"Thank you, sir," he replied politely and stepped inside the modest living room. Seconds later, Marnie skipped down the stairs in an untucked plaid shirt rolled back to the elbows which she wore over a Beatles tee shirt. Levi's and her ever present Chuck Taylors rounded out the ensemble. Her long brown hair was tied back in a ponytail.

"Aren't you a little overdressed?" she asked her friend, noting his neatly tucked in short-sleeved button-down shirt, chinos and loafers. "We're going to be runnin' around and stuff."

"I wasn't quite sure what the required attire was," he explained. "I could go home and change—"

"You look fine, Myles," said Roy, grabbing his wallet and keys. "Now let's get after it. I have some barbecue to attend to." They piled into the Fairlane, father and daughter in front with their guest in the rear as they backed out of the driveway. "Your church do any kind of stuff like this, Myles?" asked Roy, trying to make conversation.

"Well, sir, our synagogue does have some events, but they're more in line with holy days and such. And we sure don't have barbecues like this one. Thanks a lot for inviting me."

"No problem," said Marnie, shooting him a wink over her shoulder.

They arrived and parked on the far side of the church's spacious blacktopped lot, allowing the Fairlane ample space from the car next to it. Then Roy jumped out and headed for the part of the lot where the smokers had been set up while Marnie and Myles strolled around. Betty Lou and her gang, which included some boys from school and others whom she didn't know—probably from Central High—were laughing and joking at a table near the dessert tent. Betty Lou's friends didn't seem to notice them, which was fine.

Then, from the corner of her eye Marnie saw Charlotte waving madly from her seat next to Tommy Plummer at a table occupied by her parents and some of their friends. Everyone, including the adults, sipped sweet teas fetched from a huge metal urn or iced cans of RC Cola or Dr. Pepper, as no alcohol was permitted on church grounds.

Marnie and Myles slid onto the picnic bench across from Charlotte and Tommy and the introductions began. "Momma, Daddy," said Charlotte, "y'all know Marnie, and this is her friend Myles."

"Pleased to meet you, young man," said Mr. Perkins, who seemed a bit overdressed in a short-sleeved, button-down shirt and bow tie. "I don't believe we've ever seen you before. Do you belong to this church?"

"No sir," he answered respectfully. "My family attends Temple Israel across town."

"Oh, how nice," said Mrs. Perkins, a bland smile creasing her face.

"He's my guest today," said Marnie proudly. "Hey, Tommy, you know Myles, don't you?"

"We've met at school," he replied coolly. "Hi."

"Hi, Tommy," said Myles, as Marnie correctly figured this brief exchange had just exceeded the boys' total conversation for all of junior high. "I had no idea this event was so big."

"That's because everybody knows Marnie's dad is overseeing the barbecue," said Mrs. Perkins. Then to Marnie she added, "He's quite the cook. Whoever finally lands your dad will be a lucky woman."

Her husband gently nudged her in the ribs.

"Looks like the food's up," Marnie announced, searching for an escape. "Guess it's time to get in line. C'mon, Myles." They collected their paper plates, napkins and utensils and got on line. "Mrs. Perkins is always asking about Daddy," she said. "If you look over to the smokers, you can see the single women hovering nearby." Indeed, Roy was laughing with a group of ladies as he pulled the finished racks of ribs out of a smoker. "What she doesn't understand is the bad dreams and mood swings. Momma couldn't understand it, either."

"Wow," said Myles.

"What?"

"You don't mention your mom hardly ever."

"What's to mention? Truth is, I might be the only one who understands my father even halfway. The key is to know when to leave him alone."

"The war really got to him, huh?"

"More than anyone knows. That's why he needs me, Myles."

"Uh-huh."

They loaded their plates with barbecue and sides, grabbed a hunk of cornbread, and retreated to the Perkins' table. "Whatcha got there, Marnie?" asked Charlotte, who was ready to go up herself.

"Some ribs and brisket, slaw, beans, and a little potato salad. Oh Lord, the ribs are just fallin' off the bone. Daddy's done it again."

"S'matter, Myles," said Tommy, "you don't like red meat? Alls you got is a half a chicken."

"As a rule, Jews don't eat pork, Tommy," he explained quietly.

"No kidding? Well, more for me," he said and grabbed Charlotte's hand to go up.

"Now there's a charmer," observed Marnie through a mouthful of coleslaw.

"A real man of the world," added Myles.

"Although I've heard our phys ed teacher, Mr. Connor, say he's got a million-dollar arm."

"Yeah," Marnie snapped, "and a ten-cent head." They laughed together.

The rest of the meal went well, with Roy eventually joining his daughter and her friend. "How's the grub, you two?" he asked as he laid his heaping plate on the picnic table.

"Great as always, Daddy," said Marnie proudly. "You've cooked up another winner."

"I have to agree," Mr. Culpeper," Myles said, wiping barbecue sauce from his mouth with a paper napkin. "I don't think I've ever had better chicken."

"Well, that's fine," said Roy, "but don't get too full. There's lawn games to play, and I'm sure the Women's Club has whipped up a whole mess of great desserts for later on." He chatted pleasantly with Charlotte's parents about church matters and the girls' upcoming summer jobs as grocery baggers for Mr. Perkins, which would start the following Tuesday and run through August.

Predictably, Charlotte picked daintily at her inherently messy food while Tommy ate as though it was his last meal. Already a solid 6 foot and 180 pounds, he appeared to not have an ounce of fat on his body. Of course, it was in his nature to remind everyone of that, especially Myles. "Hey, Myles," he began, "you playin' any sports at Central next year?"

"I wouldn't think so," the boy replied diplomatically. "I mean, Marnie and I like to knock around a tennis ball occasionally, but she's the real athlete."

"I know," Charlotte said. "She's one of the best

softball and volleyball players in gym class. You should think of doing some sports next year, Marnie."

"Maybe. You never know," she answered coyly, her face reddening.

"There's always cheerleading," Tommy suggested. "Charlotte's trying out. Why don't you, too?"

"Nah, that's not my thing," she responded, casting a sideways glance at Betty Lou's table, whose decibel level kept rising steadily. She wondered if maybe one of them had sneaked in a flask and spiked their soft drinks. It wouldn't have surprised her, even at a church affair such as this.

The country band was now in full swing, with Roy and many of the other seated adults doing some serious toe-tapping, though nobody had yet found the courage to get up and dance in front of the temporary stage. Then, Reverend Hollis—an imposing man with a shock of white hair and a creased face that evoked images of Moses in the wilderness—hefted a megaphone and announced the commencement of the lawn games "so we can work off some of that heavenly barbecue." Adults would have a choice of playing horseshoes on four pits that had been set up, or indulge in a blueberry pie-eating contest, while the teens and children could compete in potato sack races, an egg toss, and a three-legged race.

When Myles showed little enthusiasm for partaking in these activities, citing his inappropriate attire, Marnie didn't press him, suggesting instead a second helping of food, which he eagerly accepted. She figured that good barbecue—even if it was only chicken—was not a staple of the Goldfarb household.

But Tommy, who had become increasingly

annoying in his prodding of Myles, wouldn't ease up. After returning to the table with a blue ribbon in the teen division potato sack race, he started in again. "Hey, you two," he said to Marnie and her friend, "I see y'all haven't moved off your spot. Aren't you gonna get into any of these games?"

Marnie gazed out on the field, where raw eggs were getting smashed as heavy-handed kids tried to catch them. "I don't think so," she said. "Besides, Myles has some nice clothes on—"

"Aw, c'mon," said Tommy, with a dismissive wave. "Have some fun." He thought for a second. "Tell you what, Charlotte and I personally challenge you in the three-legged race." This was news to Charlotte, who was doing her best to keep her carefully applied makeup intact.

Marnie and Myles looked at each other, and the girl could detect her friend's trepidation about being goaded into athletic competition. She was again about to beg off when Myles said, "You're on, Tommy. But here's the thing. The losing team has to serve the other dessert."

"Sounds good to *me*, big boy," said Tommy in a mocking tone. "Why don't we go over to the field?"

"Yeah, why don't we?" answered Myles with a steely countenance Marnie had never seen before.

As they walked towards the designated starting area, she said, "You sure you want to do this? I hope you're not letting Tommy get to you—"

Myles held up his hand. "Listen, Marnie, Tommy's been on my butt since we got here, if you haven't noticed, and he wasn't gonna let up unless I gave in. But that's okay, because we're gonna win this thing."

"Oh, really? How?"

"Well, for one thing, you're very athletic, but that's not the key. It's all about physics and harmony."

"Care to explain that to me?"

"Sure. The pair that wins this race has to function as a single unit. Therefore, we have to hold any unnecessary movement that would throw us off to a minimum."

"Makes sense."

"The other thing, and it really isn't scientific at all, is that I don't see how the two of them could possibly function as smoothly together as us. Even an idiot can see that Tommy and Charlotte are like oil and water. The only reason she's with him is because he's Mr. Big Man on Campus. On the other hand, I think we know how to anticipate each other's movements, and that's something that just comes naturally. You just watch."

Marnie sheepishly shrugged her shoulders. "Sounds good to me, Myles."

There were some twelve couples, half of them teens, competing in the contest. As the adult judges bound each couple's inner leg ankles and calves together with elastic bands, Myles kicked off his loafers and whispered to his partner, "First, you'll notice that I've managed it so our dominant leg is on the outside, since you're a righty and I'm a lefty. Now, what we're gonna do is, we're gonna put our arms around each other's waist and hold on tight. Then, starting with our outer legs, we're gonna call out "one, two" together the whole way through the race."

Marnie smiled. "Got it, boss."

Of course, Tommy had made sure that he and Charlotte were right next to their main adversaries, and that Tommy and Myles were barely a foot apart. As the judge got ready to shoot off a cap pistol to begin the race, Tommy leaned over and hissed, "Eat my dust, Jewboy."

"Eat *this*, Tommy," he whispered back with a tight smile.

The gun sounded, and they were off. For the course each couple would be required to sprint for 25 or so yards, take a turn around a plastic traffic cone, and make it back to the starting line. Myles and Marnie, counting off their steps like infantry soldiers, broke out of the gate to an early lead and maintained it through the first leg; predictably, Tommy had tried to dominate his partner, and Charlotte just couldn't stay in sync.

By the time they made the turn, Tommy was looking at the back of Myles's still-neatly pressed shirt and berating his partner for holding him back. He and Charlotte actually did make up some ground on the home stretch; unfortunately, they over-strode, became entangled, and went down, but not before Tommy, in a pique of desperation, flung out a hand and tried to catch the back of Myles's heel. But it was no use. Marnie and her friend crossed the finish line a full five yards ahead of anyone else in the race and were awarded the blue ribbon, which Myles pinned to Marnie's shirt like a prom corsage. "What did I tell ya?" he said proudly. "Physics and harmony was all it took."

The duo returned to the table, passing Betty Lou and company (who pointedly ignored them) and put in their order of blueberry pie topped with vanilla ice cream, which Charlotte and a muttering Tommy dutifully delivered.

Had the picnic ended there, Marnie would have

considered the day a rousing success, but someone had to come along to "spit in the punch bowl" as her daddy liked to say.

"Well, congratulations, you two," Reverend Hollis announced grandly as he took a seat across from them, Tommy having moved his date to another table. "That was quite a performance in the three-legged race." He regarded Myles with curiosity. "Marnie, I don't believe I've met your friend."

"Myles Goldfarb, Reverend," the boy said, extending his hand across the table, which was accepted. "Pleased to meet you, sir. This is a fantastic picnic. I'm so glad Marnie invited me."

"Well, we're glad to have you as our guest," said the genial clergyman. "I assume you belong to Temple Israel?"

"Why, yes, sir. Do you know our rabbi, James Wax?"

"Not personally, son, but I know of him; it's not hard to," was the Reverend's reply.

Indeed, Rabbi James Aaron "Jimmy" Wax had served in St. Louis, Missouri and Glencoe, Illinois before coming to Memphis as an associate rabbi at Temple Israel, Memphis's oldest synagogue, and rising to the rank of senior rabbi in 1954. Although classified as a reformist, he had supported the establishment of a conservative synagogue, Beth Shalom, and set about building his more moderate congregation.

But what set Wax apart from his fellow clergymen of all denominations—and what had obviously gotten Reverend Hollis's attention—was his well-publicized civil rights activism in the Memphis area.

Anti-Semitism had always been present in the South, and the Civil Rights Movement had sparked an uptick in distaste for "communist Jews" who were partly blamed for bringing about such landmark anti-segregation legislation as the Supreme Court's 1952 Brown vs. Board of Education decision, which began the initiative to outlaw Jim Crow practices in the South. This put Southern Jews in the precarious position of being shunned by their white Christian neighbors while supporting a somewhat distrusting African-American segment of society. Even his fellow Jews were wary of Wax's speaking out, citing the 1958 bombing of a Jewish temple in Atlanta as cause for conservatism. But Wax had pressed on, becoming involved not so much in public protests as working behind the scenes with groups like the Memphis Ministers Association and the Panel of American Women to promote integration and provide food for hungry black children in Memphis's segregated schools. He was also actively involved with the Memphis Committee on Community Relations, which sought a nonviolent solution to ending segregation practices in the area, especially the business sector. And though Wax didn't actively seek the limelight, his name was invariably in the news, and an annoyance to some clergy such as Reverend Hollis, who in some quarters were deemed as passive and accepting of the status quo on this controversial issue.

Myles, whose ear had become finely tuned to digs such as the one Hollis had given him, replied, "Well, sir, I don't know Rabbi Wax that well personally, and I can't say that my family is the most religious one going, but I have to give the man credit for using his influence to try to bring about a positive change. Don't you?"

Hollis seemed taken back. His eyes narrowed,

though he maintained his gregarious smile. "I think change is a good thing, yes," he said in measured tones, "but such radical adjustments in our society must be handled carefully, with restraint and patience, for they take time."

"But Reverend," countered Myles calmly, "if my math is correct, there are people around here who've been waiting over a hundred years—if you want to make the starting point the Emancipation Proclamation—for things to turn around. I'd say they've shown *a lot* of patience so far."

Marnie was sure the good reverend was about to choke on his peach cobbler as he regarded Myles's pleasantly placid visage. Then, grasping at straws, he shifted his attack to the girl. "And what do you think of *those* people, young lady?" he said, pointing a plastic fork at her Beatles tee shirt. "Do you feel *they* set a good example for the youth of America?"

Emboldened by her friend's frankness, she replied, "From everything I've heard, Reverend, and from their music, I don't see anything wrong in what the Beatles believe in. Far as I can tell, they favor equal rights for all and peace among men. Isn't that what we talk about in church every Sunday?"

The minister put his fork down and sighed. "Children, you have so, so much to learn about the world," he said, his words heavy on their ears. "But I believe your hearts are, for the most part, in the right place. Y'all have a fine rest of the day." He abruptly rose and left the table.

"Was it something I said?" asked Myles innocently.

Chapter Fourteen

The Beatles' tour dates in the Philippines had been anticipated on a scale comparable to the group's 1964 Australia visit, when it seemed the entire country had turned out to welcome them. Their recently elected president, Ferdinand Marcos, and his glamorous wife Imelda were promoting a distinctly pro-Western image and saw the Beatles' visit as a step in the direction of Western acceptance. As a result, the two concerts scheduled for the 50,000 seat Rizal Memorial Stadium were treated as a national event.

However, from the moment the Beatles' plane touched down at Manila Airport at 4:30 PM on July 3, on a remote end of the runway, the atmosphere seemed charged with anxiety. The nation's police and military forces were in a state of high alert not seen since the 1960 visit of US President Eisenhower. The Fab Four were bundled into a waiting vehicle by armed men in civilian clothes, separated for the first time on a tour from their manager and handlers. This was an especially tense moment for the boys, who were usually waived through airport security with diplomat-level immunity, and who feared some stashed bags of marijuana in their luggage would be found.

The Beatles were driven to the Philippine Navy

headquarters in Manila Harbor, escorted to a crowded press conference for the usual silly questions, and then taken aboard a luxury yacht owned by a wealthy Filipino businessman, whose son aimed to impress his friends with the celebrities his father had brought aboard. It was hot and humid, and the boat was filled with threatening-looking security guards. The musicians were understandably frightened. Only a steady stream of alcohol and a little pot supplied by their "hosts" took the edge off their anxiety.

Finally, Brian Epstein caught up with them before the boat shoved off, pitched a fit that led to their release, and had them delivered to the luxurious Manila Hotel, where they were supposed to have been taken in the first place.

Now that their quasi-abduction was out of the way, the boys were able to decompress for a while, and decided to sleep in on July 4 before their afternoon concert (except for Paul, who had sneaked out with road manager Neil Aspinall for a bit of sightseeing under cover of disguise). What the sleeping Beatles did not know was that they had been committed to attending a children's party organized by Imelda Marcos that was scheduled for 11 AM that morning at the Presidential Palace. The invitation had actually been issued while the Beatles were in Tokyo. Epstein had politely declined without informing the boys, who were routinely kept out of the loop on such matters, as invitations such as these were always crossing Epstein's desk.

Therefore, it was quite a shock when the Beatles' handlers were awakened early that morning by a pounding on the door of their suite. They opened it to find two higher-ups from the Philippine army in full dress uniform, announcing they were there to escort the Beatles to the morning reception/children's party at the palace. Understandably baffled, they tracked down Brian Epstein, who was taking a morning coffee in the hotel's restaurant. Epstein coolly responded that this event was most certainly *not* on the boys' itinerary for the day and that they not be disturbed. A subsequent telephone call from the British ambassador to the Philippines failed to change his mind.

By midmorning the hotel was in an uproar. More government officials had turned up at the Beatles' suite to argue their case for the boys' attendance at the palace event, but the more they pushed, the more the Beatles pushed back. When told that their failure to show up would offend President Marcos, John Lennon flippantly replied, "Who's he?"

And so, despite warnings that there could be serious repercussions for their actions, the Beatles did not budge from the hotel until they were taken later that afternoon to the stadium for the first of two workmanlike concerts, playing to a crowd of 30,000 in the intense heat and suffering the usual sound system and screaming fans problems. The second show at 8:30 PM that evening drew an estimated 50,000 fans, and the 80,000 total for the day set a new single day attendance record for the band.

It was between the two shows that Brian Epstein, who felt trouble was brewing, taped a message to explain the Beatles' non-appearance at the morning event, and felt that this effort on his part would diffuse the situation. He was wrong, and the backlash against the Beatles began immediately after the second concert, when their convoy of automobiles was surrounded not by a police escort, but by what seemed to be hired troublemakers, who banged on the cars' windows and started rocking the vehicles. Their terrified drivers took off and crashed through some restraining gates in order to flee the stadium's parking lot. At the same time, Brian Epstein's contrite apology over what he termed a "misunderstanding" was broadcast on the government-owned Channel 5, but for some reason, possibly deliberate, the sound was so distorted that Epstein's words were inaudible.

The Beatles barely reached the hotel ahead of an angry mob that had chased them from Rizal Stadium. A short while later a government official came to their hotel suite demanding payment of local taxes on the proceeds of the two concerts. The Beatles were horrified and angered to see television footage from the concerts was being interspersed with that of the empty seats reserved for the group at the morning reception, children crying in disappointment, and Mrs. Marcos voicing her displeasure over this most personal of insults.

Then, on the morning of July 5, things began to happen very quickly. The Beatles' man in charge of working with the Filipino tour promoters had deliberately been taken away and subjected to an intense interrogation over the group's snub of the president's wife. At the same time, death threats were being telephoned in to both the hotel and the British Embassy. All government security assigned to protect the Beatles while in the Manila Hotel suddenly evaporated. When morning edition newspapers hit the streets proclaiming the Beatles had "spit in the eyes of the first family," the decision was made to get out of Manila immediately.

The Beatles were to fly from Manila to Delhi, India for a little R&R and an opportunity for George to purchase some authentic Indian instruments for his widening interest in that style of music. But when calls were made to the downstairs desk at the hotel to check out, the staff was nowhere to be found, and there were no transport vehicles to be had. Frantically, Epstein called the airport and begged the pilot of their KLM flight to delay the takeoff. When they were finally able to secure transportation, their Filipino drivers appeared to forget the route to the airport, sometimes driving in circles as the Beatles party grew more anxious.

The airport was simply a madhouse. Porters refused to carry the Beatles' luggage, and they had to fight their way through the crowds carrying suitcases, amps and guitar cases. The escalator to the first-floor check-in area was mysteriously out of order. When they tried to make a dash for it, their hasty retreat set off an already testy horde of people who chased them as though they were criminals. Fights broke out, and those loyal to the Marcos family began spitting upon, punching and kicking the Beatles and their entourage, while those young fans still loyal to the Beatles wailed over their mistreatment at the hands of their Filipino countrymen.

In the melee it was impossible to tell the difference between armed military police and the members of the pro-Marcos group. As the Beatles made one last sprint across the tarmac to their plane, they feared being shot in the back. But even when securely inside the aircraft, whose cabin was a sweltering 90°, the ordeal wasn't over. Two Philippine military officers came aboard and removed Tony Barrow, the Beatles' press secretary, and chief roadie Mal Evans, who feared for their lives. Fortunately, they were returned to the plane a half hour later, but not before the Beatles, soaked in sweat and nervously chain-smoking cigarettes, complained long and loud about the fiasco they had just endured, and vowing it would never happen again. This led to a fight breaking out between the usually reserved Brian Epstein and the person in charge of the box office receipts.

As the plane lifted off from Manila Airport the Beatles quietly talked among themselves about ending the madness once and for all and restoring some kind of normalcy to their lives. Fortunately, they felt all that was left—as far as this tour was concerned—was a series of dates in America, a place where they had always been received well, and where they could count on their loyal fans to turn out in droves and blindly support them. It was the only thing keeping the four Beatles sane as they clung to each other in the eye of the hurricane.

Chapter Fifteen

The morning of July 8 was pretty typical for the Culpeper household. Tillie, who was on her summer schedule of Monday/Wednesday/Friday, had prepared breakfast. Marnie wolfed down her Rice Krispies and pedaled off to work at Perkins' Grocery Market, less than a mile away, her bag lunch in the Schwinn's wire basket. The store was open from 9-5 on weekdays and from 9-12 on Saturdays, but Marnie and Charlotte had the weekends off.

The routine for the girls was typical. Marnie would show up about 8:45, park her bike behind the store and chain it up, enter through the back door, clock in, and don her green, smock-like garment with Perkins Grocery Market embroidered on the left breast. She'd meet up with Charlotte, who had ridden to work with her parents, prepare the piles of folded paper bags for the day's register checkouts, and be ready for customers when the door opened at 9 AM sharp. The two cash register ladies, Janice and Debbie, had been with Mr. Perkins for many years, and although both could be a bit cranky with the girls, they were beloved by the store's loyal customers, most of whom, like them, were white and from the surrounding neighborhood.

While Mrs. Perkins would retire to an upstairs

office to work on the books and prepare the store's inventory orders, Mr. Perkins would assist the two teenaged stock boys—nephews by way of his sister—in the restocking of the shelves and unloading of new shipments that came in. There was also a deli counter run by two older women and a meat department manned by a guy named Bruce and his assistant. A colored man named Nate cleaned up at night. Other than Janice and Debbie, the girls had little interaction with the rest of the staff, which Sam Perkins, who oversaw the entire floor of the market from an upper landing, thought was just fine. His small operation ran like clockwork, and he felt that socializing had no place in the workplace. Of course, as Marnie and Charlotte worked a scant few feet from each other, they did kibitz throughout their boring day of filling shopping bags and sometimes carrying them outside for older customers. Every so often one of the seniors even gave them some small change as a tip. They also would eat lunch together downstairs in the stock room, where they had set up a small cracker box table and folding chairs. It wasn't the most exciting way to spend the summer, but for Marnie it was tax-free income to spend on makeup, clothes, and of course, Beatles records.

On this day, however, she felt something amiss with her best friend. Despite his boorish behavior at the Memorial Day picnic, Charlotte had stuck with Tommy Plummer in an on-again, off-again relationship. Marnie felt she was looking ahead to high school and getting the jump on any girls who desired the future star quarterback of the Memphis Central Warriors for themselves. But, as Marnie had seen up close, Tommy could be downright nasty and full of himself at times, and she guessed her friend and the star athlete were going through a rough patch. But since Charlotte failed to bring it up that morning or when they were alone during lunch, she let it slide.

It had been a rather slow midafternoon when the Negro boy entered the store. Marnie only noticed him because her register was closest to the "IN" door, which was plate glass, as were the panels of the store's façade. The boy looked to be in his teens, wearing a windbreaker jacket over a clean white tee shirt and jeans, with sneakers. His hair was trimmed short and his skin was smooth and mocha-colored. Marnie was sure she had seen him before, perhaps in the sports pages of the newspaper, as an athlete from one of the colored high schools in the area.

The boy walked right past Marnie, but then paused near Charlotte's station. "'Scuse me, miss," he asked, "can you tell me where I can find the condensed milk?"

She regarded him somewhat warily. "It's either in aisle two or three."

Marnie actually knew the condensed milk was in aisle one (the market only had four aisles total) but thought better of contradicting her friend, figuring the boy would find it.

What happened next occurred very quickly. Marnie had just packed two large bags for an elderly woman and was assisting her to her car when the boy, apparently exasperated in his inability to find the condensed milk, had again approached Charlotte and asked if she was sure they carried the item he sought. "Of course, I'm sure," she snapped. "Look harder." He stared at her for a long moment, then moved off again.

It was then, for whatever reason, that Charlotte went upstairs and told her father that there was a suspicious colored boy who was eyeing her. From his perch above the retail floor, Mr. Perkins scanned the aisles until he located the boy, who seemed to be moving cans around on one of the shelves. When it looked like he was going to his jacket pocket, Perkins went to the office phone and quickly dialed the number of the Memphis police.

Marnie had obliviously returned to her register, as had Charlotte, when a black and white police cruiser screeched to a halt outside the market and two young, white patrolmen jumped out, securing their billy clubs in their gun belts while putting on their black-billed peaked hats.

Those few patrons who were in Perkins' Market froze, as did the register ladies, Marnie, and Charlotte. The officers strode down one of the aisles and emerged with the boy, securely gripping him by each elbow.

"Check his pockets!" Mr. Perkins yelled down from the landing. "I think he was shoplifting!"

Marnie turned to Charlotte, who seemed to have lost all the blood in her face. She managed a "What in the Sam Hill—" before they dragged the boy outside, spread-eagled him against the front window, kicked his feet further apart, and roughly frisked him. The Negro, head down, said something to one of the officers who barked, "You just shut up, boy. What you doin' shopping in this neighborhood, anyway?"

Marnie couldn't help but stare at the scene, a mixture of fear and disgust flooding her body. For the first time since Charlotte's slumber party she felt she would vomit, and she gripped the register counter to steady herself. And then, the boy raised his head and looked straight into her eyes, his face a mask of anger and humiliation. She tried to say something but couldn't.

Suddenly, another cruiser came to an abrupt stop behind the first one and Roy Culpeper got out. Marnie rushed outside to witness her father confront the two patrolmen. "Y'all mind tellin' me what's going on here?" he calmly asked the officers.

"Sarge, we got a call from Mr. Perkins that this boy was eyeballing his daughter, sassed her, and then was goin' to steal some stuff."

Culpeper slowly removed his aviator-style sunglasses. "So y'all dragged him out here for all to see and frisked him?"

"Yessir," replied one of them whose nameplate read Mathews.

"And did he have any stolen items on his person?"

"Nossir, but he backtalked us and—"

"Let him go."

The officers looked at each other with incredulity. "You sure, Sarge?" the other one said.

"You got grits in your ears, Stevens? I said turn him loose."

The officers released their grip on the boy. "I'll take it from here, men," said Roy. "No need to file a report. I'll discuss this with Lieutenant Sutter myself."

"Okay, Sarge, if you say so," said the one named Stevens. The officers, clearly embarrassed, returned to their vehicle, started the engine, and sharply pulled out into traffic.

Roy turned to face his daughter. "Now, you git," he growled, and Marnie hurried back inside. She watched from her register as Roy brought the boy over to his car and leaned back against it as they talked. The boy was clearly emotional and a couple times raised his arms in a gesture of frustration. Finally, Roy put his hand on the boy's shoulder, said some words that seemed to calm him, put him in the back seat of the patrol car, and drove off.

"Serves him right," sniffed Charlotte. "That boy was disrespectful to me," she added so all could hear.

"All right then, everyone," called down Mr. Perkins from the landing. "Show's over. Let's all get back to work, now." But for the rest of the afternoon, Marnie could not get the images she had witnessed out of her mind or stop wondering what her father was going to do to that boy. Hardly a word passed between her and Charlotte for the rest of the day.

Marnie rode home, her insides a jumble of mixed emotions, until she reached her house. The same police cruiser her father had driven earlier was parked out front. She entered the side door to the kitchen to find Roy Culpeper, still in uniform, at the round table. The colored boy from the store was next to him, his head resting on his forearms atop the table's surface. And next to him sat his mother, a reassuring hand on his shoulder. That's when it all clicked for Marnie.

"Why we got to go through all this, Momma?" the boy was mumbling through his tears. "When you called and said you needed some condensed milk for Mr. Culpeper's cake, I figured I'd go to the closest market and…and…"

Tillie stroked her son's hair. "Not your fault,

Marcus. That's just the way things are. Now stop your cryin' and act like a man."

Marnie, at a loss for words, managed, "How did you know to show up, Daddy?"

"It came over the radio," he said matter-of-factly. "I was actually out getting lunch and saw the black-and-white fly by me goin' the other way. When I realized who it was in the car, I hung a U-turn, because those two hotheads are nothin' but trouble. Sorry I couldn't have gotten there sooner."

"Mr. Culpeper, is this gonna affect me signin' up for the Marines?" said Marcus, who had finally sat up, revealing bloodshot eyes.

"No," Roy said. "There was no arrest, so it never happened. You can still join up, if that's what you want." He spoke in a manner that was supposed to be comforting to the boy, but Marnie could sense some uneasiness in her father's face. "By the way, Marcus, in case you haven't figured it out, this is my daughter, Marnie."

"Pleased to meet you," he said, regaining his composure. "Momma has told me a lot about you."

"Hi," she said quietly.

"Well then," said Roy, pushing his chair back from the kitchenette table, "I'm gonna run Tillie and Marcus home, drop off the patrol car and come back here. You'll heat up the dinner Tillie's prepared?"

"You bet, Daddy," said Marnie.

"Fine. Then I'll see you in an hour or so."

The girl gave Marcus a quick handshake, and then hugged her housekeeper long and hard.

"I'll see you Friday, honey," said the woman, and they left.

Marnie sat for a few minutes at the table, then went upstairs to her room, put *Rubber Soul* on the turntable and contemplated the complexities of human behavior. After the album's last track "Run for your Life" ended, she headed downstairs, set up the table and heated up the oven. Tillie had made one of Roy's favorites, barbecued spaghetti, using some leftover pulled pork shoulder which she mixed with a spicy-sweet sauce worthy of any restaurant table on Beale Street and ladled over pasta noodles. It wouldn't be as good heated up a couple hours later than normal, but this hadn't been a normal day.

A half hour beyond what she'd expected, Roy, in street clothes, pulled into the driveway, garaged the Fairlane, and wearily trudged into the house, plopping himself down on a kitchenette chair. "That smells really good, baby girl," he said quietly. "Can't wait to dig in."

"You want a sweet tea with that, Daddy?" she said, removing a Corningware bowl from the oven with a couple of potholders.

"Nah, I think I'd like a Budweiser tonight."

Marnie looked at him for a second. "Sure thing," she said, reaching into the refrigerator for a cold one. She took a bottle opener from the silverware drawer, flipped off the cap and handed it to her father, who accepted it with a nod and drank half of it down. She put the plate of spaghetti in front of him and he methodically stuck a fork into the pile and started twirling it. Then she got herself seated and said, "Anything you'd like to tell me, Daddy?"

He stopped twirling his spaghetti, and even managed a faint smile. "I just can't get anything by you, can I?" he said. "Ah well, it's nothing, really. I dropped off Tillie and Marcus and drove back to HQ and of course Sutter was waiting for me. Apparently those two hardass wanna-be officers went straight to him and complained, so he had to question me as to why I 'interfered' in an arrest and 'embarrassed' two of Memphis's finest in public. So, I explained that the boy hadn't done anything, that your friend had just overreacted for Lord knows why, and that the matter wasn't worth pursuing."

"Did Lieutenant Sutter know Marcus's mother worked for us?"

"Not at first, but I told him and that allowed me to vouch for his honesty. I also told him that the colored boy his men were so hot and bothered to arrest was days away from enlisting in the Marine Corps to defend his country."

"What did he say to that?"

Roy's lips became tight, and he started to twirl his spaghetti again. "He said, 'Well, maybe the commies will take care of him for us.'"

Chapter Sixteen

Journalist Maureen Cleave had first met the Beatles in 1963 when she was in her late twenties and writing a column on pop music for London's *Evening Standard* newspaper. Well educated and attractive, she had grown up in India, where her father was a major in the British Indian Army. After graduating from Oxford, she had pursued a career in journalism, and her youth and interest in the changing culture of British society—most notably the immersion its of young people in rock and roll—led to her position with the *Evening Standard*, and her subsequent interest in a new group from Liverpool that was gaining notoriety.

The result of this meeting was a published feature in February of that year under the headline "**Why the Beatles Create All That Frenzy**" which helped introduce the group, whose fame had been restricted mostly to the Merseyside area of Liverpool, to a wider audience. She made it quite clear that the Beatles' sound was unique and that they bore watching; also mentioned was what she referred to as a "purposely scruffy" look highlighted by their French-influenced hairstyles. She was also perceptive enough to pick up on their irreverent manner and self-confidence as well as their overall intelligence.

The article went beyond the usual frothy teen idol-styled portraits of the time, and the band members appreciated that she gave them a kind of respect not usually bestowed upon pop stars, at least not in mainstream media forums like the *Evening Standard*. As a result, Cleave became a trusted confidante and was allowed into the inner sanctum of the group for a 3-part series called "The Year of the Beatles" in 1964. And when the Beatles flew to America for their landmark first appearances, Cleave was on the plane with them. No member of the press media had a better relationship with the boys.

Now, in 1966, she had the idea to present the Beatles not as a single entity, but as four diverse personalities who had blended their talents to become the predominant force in rock and roll and cultural icons to youth. She decided to interview each one individually, as well as Brian Epstein, to reveal what made each one tick as they were growing from boys to men. The overall theme was to be "How a Beatle Lives." As Cleave was to find out, the four lads from Liverpool were, indeed, unique personalities.

Ringo was portrayed as a man of simple tastes whose childhood illnesses and hardscrabble existence had made him desirous of the material possessions of a rock and roll hero that validated his self-image and gave him security: sports cars, various collections, a house in the country, and a loving wife and son. When questioned on matters outside the Beatles, such as the world's problems, he voiced his displeasure with the nuclear arms race and world famine, and even suggested that an alien visit might give earthlings a better perspective on life. In essence, Ringo seemed to truly appreciate his bandmates as brothers and was content in his Beatle life.

George Harrison, always characterized in the media as the "quiet Beatle," came off as a lot more outspoken, strong-willed and independent than what was believed. Although he enjoyed the trappings of his fame, his exposure to other cultures, most notably Indian, had broadened his horizons, and his new wife Patti had further fueled his desire to see what else was out there. Even at this somewhat early juncture, he was becoming tired of the whole Beatle thing, and had come to detest the early moptop image, which he viewed as a compromise to help get the band's foot in the door of the entertainment business.

When Cleave pressed him on world issues, the quiet Beatle did not hold back. He strongly denounced the war in Vietnam and the praise heaped upon the victors of World War II in Great Britain. This led to his distrust of all authority figures, including those in the clergy.

Organized religion had no part in the life of George Harrison as of 1966, though he refused to be cast as a "non-spiritual" person. He told Cleave that religion "…falls flat on its face. All this 'love thy neighbor' and none of them (clergy leaders) are doing it…Why can't we bring all this out in the open? Why is there all this stuff about blasphemy? If Christianity's as good as they say it is, it should stand up to a bit of discussion."

One would think these words would have ruffled some feathers in England when George's interview piece ran in the *Evening Standard*, but it hardly caused a blip on the radar, as British society in general was far more used to opinionated material in the press.

John Lennon, whom Cleve had grown closest to over the years, presented her greatest challenge as far as defining him to the public. It seemed to her that the leader of the Beatles was a jumble of contradictions. He could be hard-driving or lazy, blue-collar or upper-crust, childish or charming, easy-going or bitingly sarcastic. However, one thing was clear: this former poor student had a thirst for knowledge, though he sought it haphazardly and from a variety of sources. Lennon also had far more of a tendency for introspection and self-examination than his bandmates, as evidenced most recently in songs like "Help!," "Nowhere Man" and "In My Life."

He was also tired of answering what he felt were "soft" questions during the much-hated interviews for teen magazines and press conferences, such as how often he washed his Beatle haircut. If Cleave was willing to go deeper, so would Lennon. Brian Epstein and the public in general would just have to live with it. Thus, when the subject of religion came up, the sharp- tongued Lennon did not hold back. John had been raised in a decidedly Christian environment by his aunt Mimi and attended Sunday school, even participating in the church choir and Bible study activities. He had said even before the Cleave interview that his aunt only sent him to church out of a sense of duty to give him what was considered a normal British upbringing, but that this forced inclusion had given him the opportunity to decide for himself if organized religion was for him.

After he had left his teens (along with the church) for a life of fame and fortune, Lennon had begun to think about spirituality, just as his bandmate George, though he came at it from a different angle. As John saw it, charismatic religious leaders such as Jesus Christ had a lot in common with modern rock and roll icons such as Elvis Presley (or the Beatles) in that they were the objects of mass devotion, were extremely influential, and were thus targets of others who misunderstood or even hated what they represented. Jesus, especially, was an intriguing figure to Lennon, who believed him to be in tune with the feelings of others and who preached peace and love. Of course, the parallels between this long-haired man who inspired the masses and his own Beatle bandmates were not lost upon the extremely perceptive Lennon.

And so, when Maureen Cleave asked John Lennon what he thought about the institution of Christianity in the world, he said, "Christianity will go. It will vanish and shrink. I needn't argue about that; I'm right and I will be proved right. *We're* more popular than Jesus now. Jesus was all right but his disciples were thick and ordinary. It's them twisting it that ruins it for me." When John made these comments, he was obviously basing it upon the culture he knew best—that of England, which he predicted would see Christianity go into decline as the years passed. Perhaps he was drawing upon the phenomenon of adulation that was blindly heaped upon him and the other Beatles, or the tangible fact that their 1964 film *A Hard Day's Night* had earned more critical acclaim and made much more money than the 1965 biblical epic *The Greatest Story Ever Told*. Or maybe it was the experience of having sick or crippled children brought to the Beatles' dressing room before concerts in hopes that the touch of a Beatle could actually heal them or improve their lives, something that he had a hard time dealing with.

Lennon honestly felt that rock and roll had risen to religion-like status with the young, and that the songs and their lyrics, of the Beatles and others, were a new kind of scripture, transmitted to the masses by the rock stars who acted as messiahs or gurus, their ever-growing concert events taking on the flavor of old time open-air religious revivals.

Cleave's subsequent interview with Paul McCartney proved to be about what she expected. The neatly dressed, impeccably groomed diplomat of the group was well-spoken, eager for knowledge like his friend John, and proud to be a Briton. Indeed, he relished the fact that his band had helped bring about a cultural shift in England's young people, whom he felt were more open to change than Americans, who had, to that time, equated short hair with men and long hair with women. But unlike John or George, he glossed over world matters and when his interview with Cleave ran in the paper at the end of the spring, the Beatles were too hard at work finishing *Revolver* and readying themselves for the first leg of their summer tour to really care.

However, with the United States tour coming up, Tony Barrow, the Beatles' publicist, felt that these intelligent, well-written interviews could be put to further use by offering them to the editor of the American teen magazine *Datebook*, and with Brian Epstein's blessing, he did just that.

* * *

The Beatles' European/Eastern tour of 1966 had ended disastrously, so much so that they needed time away to rest and recharge before venturing again to the United States. Manager Epstein had been left so drained by the terrible time in Manila that he went to recuperate at a resort spa in Wales. It was time for everyone in the Beatles entourage to decompress.

But this was not to be. Scant days before they were to leave for the States, the *Datebook* article, which had taken Cleave's *Evening Standard* texts and edited them down for effect, hit the newsstands of America.

And all hell broke loose.

Chapter Seventeen

Marnie had been hearing various tracks from *Revolver*, the Beatles' new album, since mid-July, most notably the lovely, Beach Boys-like ballad, "Here, There, and Everywhere," the haunting "Eleanor Rigby," and the jovial sing-along "Yellow Submarine," but she would not experience the full effect of the album until the first week of August when, after putting aside necessary funds from her job at Perkins' Market, she pedaled downtown on a Saturday to A. Schwab's department store and purchased a brand-new copy.

When Marnie listened to her Beatles records, she liked to imagine the boys singing those songs onstage, as in the *Ed Sullivan Show* days, or maybe in *A Hard Day's Night* or *Help!* And when Paul and John sang duet-style numbers like "I Don't Want to Spoil the Party," or more recently, "We Can Work It Out," she pictured them alone, sitting on chairs with acoustic guitars, facing each other, perfecting the harmonies as they went along, best buddies creating magic together.

But when she retreated to her room that Saturday (Myles was at Temple, and not available as he had been for *Rubber Soul*) she was both amazed and confused at what she heard. Over and over she played the LP, happy that her dad was out fishing with Cecil for the day, or he'd think she was crazy. Finally, around 4 PM she could bear it no longer and called her friend.

"What's up, Buttercup?" he said flippantly.

"I've gotta come over," she replied seriously. "I got *Revolver* today, and I've listened to it like a hundred times, but you've just gotta hear it for yourself."

"It's that good?"

"That's just it, Myles," she answered, "I don't really know."

"Hmm," he said. "Well, my mom and dad are gonna grill some burgers. We'll listen to the album and have a bite to eat. Sound good?"

"Sounds great," she replied, realizing that all she had on hand was enough fixings to make a grilled cheese sandwich. "I'll be right over." Carefully she placed the album, still in its neatly-slitted plastic wrapping, in her bike's basket and took off through the oppressive August heat to the Goldfarbs' blessedly air-conditioned house.

Once inside, Marnie was greeted by Mr. and Mrs. Goldfarb. He was an older version of Myles, except that his hair was shorter. And even though he carried more weight, she saw the angular shoulders of her friend. Mrs. Goldfarb was shapely, had kind of reddish brown hair formed into a stylish bouffant, and wore a sundress on this sweltering day. She also carried a highball glass in her hand with a napkin held in place by a rubber band around its bottom. "So nice to have you over, Marnie," said the woman gaily. "Will you two be joining us on the patio for some hamburgers?"

"Actually, Mom, it's a little hot out there for me,"

Myles said. "Besides, Marnie has a record for us to listen to. Is it okay if we set up a couple snack tables the living room where it's cooler?"

"As long as you don't spill any ketchup on the carpet," Myles's dad said.

"Or Coke," his wife added, who was most definitely not drinking Coke herself.

"No problem, Mom," Myles said. "Just call us when it's ready."

The adults went outside. Marnie could hear charcoal briquettes being emptied into a barbecue grill and the sound of a radio being switched on.

"It's just as well," Myles remarked. "They're into Frank Sinatra and Barbra Streisand and that kind of stuff. I'm not sure they'd appreciate this."

"I'm not sure *I* do," Marnie said, handing over the album sleeve.

"Wow, what have we here?" Myles said, examining the cover, which was definitely different, even when compared to the dreary, elongated Beatle images of *Rubber Soul*.

Looking for something completely outside the norm (though not as radical as the previously rejected "butcher" cover) the Beatles had enlisted an old friend from their Hamburg days, Klaus Voorman, a musician with a flair for art, to create a cover that would reflect the flavor of the music on the disc inside. Voorman had come up with a black and white ink format that featured the four heads of the bandmates, none with a smile, framing a collage of small black and white photos of them which seemed to be emerging from their hair. The name of the group did not appear on the cover. The result was visually striking and the Beatles had loved it. Again, they were leading the way in the pop world, aiming to start a trend that would elevate album covers to an art form.

"What you think?" Marnie said, after her friend had a minute to take it all in.

"I think it's groovy."

"Yeah, I kinda think so, too."

Myles gently removed the LP from its sleeve and warmed up the stereo. "So, how's life over at the market?" he asked nonchalantly. "Have things smoothed out any?"

Marnie frowned and shook her head. She had confided in Myles about the terrible day in July with Tillie's son, and it had made her feel better, at least for a time. "I guess it's okay," she replied, "but there's definitely been a change between me and Charlotte. That day I saw something in her that, I don't know, made me a little scared about her. I know that since then, we just keep it light when we talk. And her parents are still nice to me, but it seems a little phony."

"She still going out with Tommy Touchdown?"

"As far as I know, but that's another thing. She feels I don't like him—"

"Which you don't."

"Yeah, but it's not like I've ever come right out and said it to her."

Myles laughed. "Marnie, I don't know if you realize this, but you're not so good at hiding your feelings."

"I guess. Anyway, I'm hoping it gets better by the end of summer. How is *your* summer job going?"

Myles sighed, the LP still in his hands. "I don't know. When my dad first told me I could have a job with his company as what he called an "office assistant," I thought it sounded cool. I mean, I'd be in an air-conditioned place all day instead of mowing lawns or working as a camp counselor with a bunch of screaming brats. Basically, what I am is go-fer, getting stuff from the mailroom, bringing people coffee or lunch, things like that. And I get to wear a tie every day, so it gives the appearance that I'm some kind of mature guy. But to tell you the truth, I don't like what I see about the whole business world deal. My dad makes a great salary so we can live in this big house and my mom can basically do nothing all day—" he nodded towards the patio, where his parents were chatting pleasantly—"but I can see there's a lot of pressure on him. You know, he flies all over the country getting new accounts, reaching his quotas or whatever, and it really wipes him out. When he's home for a while, like right now, he just lays around. He's got zero desire to do anything with *me*, that's for sure. So, when he tells me that this summer job is good training for me, and that I'll be ready to just slide into a business career when I graduate from some Ivy League college, I just yes him to death. Truth is, a career in business is the *last* thing I'd want."

"What *would* you want, then?"

"I don't know," he said honestly.

"Burgers are ready!" Mr. Goldfarb called from outside. "Get 'em while they're hot, you two!"

Myles gently laid the LP on the turntable. "We'll listen to this record eventually," he joked. "Let's go pick up our food, and then they'll leave us alone for a while."

They went outside to the patio and loaded their

Chinet plates with somewhat overdone burgers and store-bought potato salad and coleslaw. Marnie also laid a slice of tomato and a few lettuce leaves on her meat in an attempt to eat something healthy that evening. Myles grabbed a couple Cokes from the refrigerator (Marnie had only now begun to drink it again, having switched to 7-Up or Dr. Pepper as she recovered from the trauma of the slumber party) and they set up the metal TV snack trays.

They settled in, side-by-side on the living room couch, the snack tables before them, as *Revolver* began to play. "Let's hear it all the way through while we're eating," suggested Myles. "Then we can listen to it again, song by song, and say what we think."

"Sounds good to me."

Thirty-five minutes later, the album had finished and their plates were clean. "Dad overcooked the meat again. Sorry," said Myles with a smile. "Not everyone can barbecue like Roy Culpeper. By the way, does he know where you are?"

"Yeah, I left a note on the kitchen table. He should be just gettin' home about now from fishing. By the time he and Cecil divvy up all the fish they caught and he packs 'em in the deep freeze in the garage, I'll be on my way home."

They moved to the floor for the second playing of the album and every song brought forth intense discussion. The first track, "Taxman," was notable in that George Harrison, not the famed Lennon-McCartney songwriting tandem, had penned the lyrics of this bitterly sarcastic diatribe against the tax laws in Britain that were, apparently, robbing George and his mates of their musical royalties. That George, who had kind of stayed in the background in the group's early days, had been given the honor of leading off an album was interesting in itself.

"Eleanor Rigby," the two teens agreed, was both sad and brilliant.

"Didja notice the only instruments is like a string quartet?" asked Myles. "The Beatles aren't even playing on the song, or singing, except Paul. Really weird."

"It gets weirder," said Marnie as the next track, another George Harrison effort, began. "Love You To" brought to the forefront Harrison's interest in Indian music that had been previewed in "Norwegian Wood" on *Rubber Soul*. This song was a full-blown Indian treatment ("the kind you hear in an Indian restaurant," mused Myles, who had apparently visited one in New York as a child), and was so foreign sounding that Mrs. Goldfarb, who was passing through the living room on the way to freshen up her vodka Collins, stopped and said, "Who's that?"

"It's the Beatles," replied Marnie.

"The *Beatles?* You're kidding," she said before moving on.

Finally, with "Here, There, and Everywhere" the teens could exhale. "A nice romantic song. Perfect for slow dancing," Marnie said. Myles agreed, declaring it "like one of the old Paul songs."

"Yellow Submarine," the next number, was a lot of fun, with Ringo, who was usually given country-style song covers like "Act Naturally" and "Honey Don't," spreading his wings as a vocalist in a goofy tune filled with sound effects that made one think he was at some kind of underwater hotel party.

"I feel like you'll be singing this all the way home," Myles mused to his friend. He was partly right—she'd been humming the chorus all the way to his house that afternoon.

The first Lennon song, "She Said She Said" was so different lyric-wise that they actually listened to it twice more in a row.

"I know what it's like to be dead"? Marnie questioned. "What in tarnation does *that* mean?"

"Maybe someone who came out of a coma?" Myles guessed.

"Could be. But what are they doin' writing songs about comas, anyway?" she asked.

"Good point."

Side Two was just as perplexing. It began with a cheery Paul offering called "Good Day Sunshine," which Marnie had actually heard played on the radio in previous weeks; but its follow-up, "For No One," was a moody, sad song in which Paul told the story of a relationship that had ended badly, a really *adult*-sounding tune that kind of canceled out the good vibes of the previous song. Myles wondered aloud if that had been the Beatles' plan in putting the songs back-to-back, and if so, why?

"I Want to Tell You," George's unprecedented third feature track, including a repetitive, purposely off-key piano riff that Marnie and Myles found innovative, and the next number, "Got to Get You into My Life," a Paul rocker, featured for the first time on a Beatles album a song with full brass backing.

But it was the last track that Marnie had told Myles he'd better prepare himself for, because "It's so weird you won't believe it."

Thus, Myles pulled his knees up to his chest, rested his chin on them, closed his eyes, and carefully listened again to "Tomorrow Never Knows." After an initial droning chord, it seemed like layers upon layers of sound were being laid atop Ringo Starr's hypnotic, repetitive drumming pattern: tape loops that seemed to go back and forth, high-pitched laughter and something that sounded like a herd of elephants. But above all was the voice of John Lennon, who sounded as if he were singing through a megaphone.

When the song ended, Myles simply said, "Again."

Marnie popped up and reset the needle, and the song played out.

"Again."

After the fourth time around, Myles finally opened his eyes. "It's like…you're in some faraway place, and there are these people chanting… kind of religious… telling you to *'lay down your mind'* and *'relax and float downstream'* and *'surrender to the void,'* like John's a holy man or something, and he's preaching from some mountaintop.

"And then there's that 'dying' thing again, like in the other song, where the girl said she knew what it's like to die. In this one he says, *'It is not dying'*."

They looked at each other, as if what they had stumbled upon here in an air conditioned, shag-carpeted living room in Memphis, Tennessee was some strange message that held the meaning of life, or at least something important. It was all too much.

"Want a Moon Pie? We have some in the fridge," Myles said, breaking the stalemate.

"Sure."

He fetched a couple of the round dessert sandwiches, oversized graham crackers stuffed with marshmallow and dipped in milk chocolate, and handed her one, along with an icy glass of milk. "My question is," he said as he chewed, "what are they getting at with all this? What does it all mean?"

"You got me," she replied, trying to pry marshmallow off the roof of her mouth with her tongue. "And can you see them playing any of the songs at the concert?"

"Maybe. One or two. But I wouldn't be surprised if they just stuck to the older stuff."

"Me neither." She paused. "They're changing, Myles. And I have a feeling it's gonna go on like this. Who knows what they're gonna come up with next? Tell you what, it's kinda scary. I mean, part of me wants them to stay in the same, but I guess that's unrealistic, huh?"

"Everyone changes, Marnie."

"I guess." Then she brightened. "Man, I am so looking forward to that concert, Myles. I'm counting the days."

"And your dad is okay with you going with me?"

"Sure. I mean, your dad or mom is dropping us off at the Coliseum and picking us up. And who knows? Maybe Daddy will be on police detail that night at the Coliseum. Maybe he'll even get us backstage to meet the Beatles!"

"Yeah, sure," Myles said, slurping the rest of his milk.

"Well, I can dream, can't I?" she said with a wink. "After all, tomorrow never knows."

Chapter Eighteen

Arthur Unger was a World War II veteran who, like Roy Culpeper, had taken advantage of the G.I. Bill to put himself through college, earning a degree in journalism. His desire was to begin an entertainment journalism magazine and *Datebook* was his creation. In 1964 and '65, he had gotten to know the Beatles somewhat, traveling with them on their American tours and even publishing special issues of *Datebook* entitled "All about the Beatles."

However, unlike teen magazines such as the *Tiger Beat* that Marnie and her friends read and later cut to shreds for the teen idol photos, Unger, as editor, like to delve into serious social and political topics as well. He sympathized with oppressed minority groups in America, and it was not unusual for *Datebook* to feature stories on Jim Crow policies or voting laws alongside traditional pop star profiles.

As he became more accepted by the Beatles camp, Unger and his magazine were occasionally fed exclusive quotes or scoops. (*Datebook* had actually broached the issue of segregation with, of all people, Ringo Starr, who termed the institution "rubbish" and vowed the Beatles would never play before audiences that were not integrated). And so, when Beatles publicist Tony Barrow offered the *Evening Standard* texts of Maureen Cleave to Unger for use in his magazine, he readily accepted, figuring correctly that the material included therein would stir up controversy, and thus sell more magazines. Barrow simply figured the deal would keep the Beatles in the limelight leading into their 1966 summer tour. He couldn't have been more correct.

The aptly named "Shout out" issue of *Datebook*, which hit American newsstands at the end of July, featured a photo of Paul McCartney in the familiar Beatle outfit of jacket and tie, singing during a live performance. But it was the textual sidebars next to Paul's handsome face that jumped off the cover:

Paul McCartney: "It's a lousy country where anyone black is a dirty nigger."

John Lennon: "I don't know which will go first—rock n' roll or Christianity."

To make sure nobody missed this issue—of what was to this point a mildly popular magazine—Unger mailed advance copies to some of the more outspoken deejays in the South and waited for the bomb he'd constructed to detonate. It was a short fuse.

On Sunday, July 31, two disc jockeys at radio station WAQY in Birmingham, Alabama, bit hard on the hook Unger had set. Like many AM stations across the US geared to young people, WAQY (also known as "Wacky Radio") allowed deejay Tommy Charles to incorporate current topics into his Top-40 format morning show. Thus, the *Datebook* article provided a treasure trove of incendiary material that both Charles, a forerunner of "shock jock" deejays everywhere, and his partner Doug Layton, could use to rile up listeners in the conservative Bible Belt of the South, and in so doing carve out a name for themselves and their radio station.

After discussing it between themselves, the two deejays decided to announce on their morning show that they would cease to play Beatles music. When they explained their stance on the air, the station was inundated with phone calls, overwhelmingly supporting their decision and condemning Lennon, whose statements Charles called "absurd and sacrilegious." He then added fuel to the fire by saying, "Something ought to be done to show them they cannot get away with this sort of thing."

Whether the actions of these men were driven by a deep sense of religious morality was questionable. What was indisputable to their listeners was that the Beatles—most notably John Lennon (as Paul's equally dramatic quotes were, mysteriously, more or less ignored)—had crossed a line, and that there had to be consequences.

Radical as they were, the remarks of Charles and Layton might have been limited to the Birmingham area had not the local bureau chief of the United Press International news service been driving in his car that morning with the radio tuned to WAQY and heard the fireworks. Certain that this was huge news, he filed it to UPI, and the story was immediately sent out to newspapers in America, where it spread from South to North.

This was an opportunity for conservative Americans who had disliked the Beatles and all they represented to finally pull them from the spotlight, and they jumped on it.

Now firmly at the forefront of the "Ban the Beatles" movement, Charles and Layton upped the ante, announcing plans to hold a "Beatle Burning" in the near future, in which those who possessed any Beatle records, magazines, clothing, or related paraphernalia were to bring these items to a designated drop-off site for a retaliatory bonfire. Charles said events such as these would remind the Beatles they were not godlike and that it was time somebody put them in their place.

Other radio stations across the US quickly fell in line. KZEE in Weatherford, Texas, "damned their songs to eternity." KCBN in Reno, Nevada, broadcast hourly anti-Beatles editorials. Whether it was Kentucky, Ohio, Georgia, Mississippi, South Carolina, Utah, Michigan, Connecticut, or even upstate New York, the anti-Beatle movement was clearly gaining traction.

At first, Brian Epstein, as well as the Beatles themselves, laughed it off, reasoning that in order to burn Beatles records, people would have to *buy* them first. But as the days passed and the furor grew, Epstein became nervous, especially when representatives of organized religion joined in the frenzy. A pastor in Cleveland, Ohio actually threatened to excommunicate any members of his congregation who attended the Beatles concert scheduled there on August 14, and the Pope issued a statement categorizing Lennon's words as profanity. The governments of South Africa and Spain went so far as to issue official condemnations.

With a US tour only days away, Epstein now realized some immediate damage control was necessary. Still in a fragile mental state from the Manila fiasco and sick with the flu, Epstein flew to

New York City to hold a press conference at the Americana Hotel, having been advised that a cancellation of the US tour would cost the Beatles millions of dollars. Carefully, the Beatles' manager read the following statement:

"The quote which John Lennon made to a London columnist nearly three months ago has been quoted and represented entirely out of context. Lennon is deeply interested in religion. What he said and meant was that he was astonished that in the last fifty years the Church of England, and therefore Christ, had suffered a decline in interest. He did not mean to boast about the Beatles' fame. He meant to point out that the Beatles' effect appeared to be, to him, a more immediate one upon certain of the young generation."

It was Epstein's hope that this "clarification" of John Lennon's statements, coupled with enthusiasm over the Beatles' new singles "Yellow Submarine" and "Eleanor Rigby," which were getting airplay from those stations who had not shunned the group, would lead to public acclaim of *Revolver* and a lucrative US tour.

There was a problem with this optimistic strategy, however. John Lennon had told Epstein that he would not back down from what he said.

The Beatles would depart London on August 11, as planned, and hope for the best.

Chapter Nineteen

Marnie usually hated Mondays. Even now during the summer, when she had the luxury of sleeping an extra half-hour, the thought of another boring day bagging groceries was deflating. Nevertheless, when her alarm clock went off, she rolled to her side, pressed the button to get the record player going, and shuffled off to the bathroom. *Revolver* was now the morning album of choice, as she was still trying to figure it out. As she tugged on her Beatles tee shirt, she studied its reflection in the bathroom mirror. The boys were in a posed photo from around 1963, in their gray collarless suits. All of them were smiling. She thought, *they look so young.*

Tying up her Chuck Taylors, Marnie wondered why Tillie hadn't barked at her yet to hurry up. Maybe because Daddy was sleeping in the other room; he would be on night shift the next two weeks. She descended the stairs after crossing off another day on her calendar—only eleven left until the concert—and bounded into the kitchen. "Hey, Tillie, is something wrong? You didn't call for me—"

The housekeeper was standing, her back to the sink. Her eyes looked red, her face a mask of worry. Silently, she pointed at the kitchenette table where the *Memphis Commercial Appeal* lay splayed out next to

Marnie's bowl of cereal. The girl approached slowly, pulled out her chair, sat down, and raised the newspaper to her face. The headline hit her like a slap: **"Lennon Says Beatles More Popular Than Jesus**." For many moments, Marnie was speechless. There was a head shot of John, probably from around 1965, directly underneath the headline.

Before she could say anything or even begin reading the article Tillie said, "Child, I *told* you those bugs were up to no good—"

"Not now, Tillie," she said quietly. "Please." Numbly, Marnie read the article through twice, learning about the Birmingham boycott and its spread to other states.

"Your cereal's gettin' soggy," said Tillie finally.

"I'm not hungry, thank you."

She grabbed her paper lunch bag off the counter, rolled up the newspaper, and carried them both out back, depositing them in her bicycle basket. With a heavy heart, she started pedaling towards Perkins' Market. Once there, she hoped to avoid the owner, but of course Mr. Perkins, his pencil-thin mustache twitching, was there to intercept her as she came through the back door.

"Marnie, have you seen today's paper?" he said with a coldness she'd not heard before.

"Yes, sir," she mumbled.

"And *still* you wore that shirt to work?"

Marnie looked down. She'd been so stunned at the house she hadn't even thought about changing. Perhaps that was why two different cars had honked their horn at her on the way over? "Sorry, Mr. Perkins," she said. "My smock will cover it."

"Make sure it does. And I'll have to ask you that going forward, you wear something else when you come to work in my store."

"Yes, sir."

Charlotte didn't provide much of a relief. "What in the world was he *thinkin'?"* she hissed across the aisle when Marnie took her place at the counter.

"I don't know," Marnie responded truthfully. It was going to be a long day.

She rode home, not hungry despite hardly touching her lunch, plodded up to her room and turned on the record player. *Revolver* was still on the turntable, which she removed and replaced with *Meet the Beatles*, their first album. She needed a reminder of happier times.

The phone rang around 7 PM, as Marnie was heating up pork chops Tillie had prepared for her. "Hi," said Myles.

"Hey."

"I take it you've heard?"

"Yeah, I read the *Commercial Appeal* this morning."

"It's in the *Scimitar,* too. At the office it was all over the place. We get newspapers from a lot of the cities. A lot of stations are banning Beatles records, mainly in the South. The Carolinas are really going crazy over this. And get this: there was an article in a newspaper in Birmingham that announced there's gonna be a big get-together to pulverize like hundreds of Beatles records in a tree grinding machine. When the records are reduced to dust they're gonna put it in a box and present it to the Beatles when they get to Memphis."

"Oh, no."

"Oh, yes. Not only that, there's gonna be these bonfires where people drop off all their Beatles records and stuff and they put 'em in a big pile and torch 'em."

"You mean, like those newsreels we saw in history class about the Nazi book burnings during the war?"

"*Exactly* like it. I don't mind telling you, it's a little scary. And I even saw one article that said the Klan was giving its support to all this."

"*They're* getting involved?"

"Oh, yeah," he said bitterly. "This is right up their alley."

"Well," she said, "it's already begun around here. Tillie started in with her 'sinful, sinful' stuff and I got the cold shoulder from Charlotte and her parents."

"How about your dad?"

"Haven't seen him yet. He's on night shift the next two weeks. Maybe that's a blessing."

"But how do *you* feel about all this, Marnie?"

She thought hard. "I don't know what to think, Myles. I can't believe that he would actually say something running down Jesus Christ. There's gotta be more to it, something I'm not getting."

"Well, when you've got it figured out, let me in on it, because I'm clueless here."

"Okay."

"And keep your chin up. This will blow over."

"I'm not so sure it will," she said. "At least not before the 19th."

Chapter Twenty

John Lennon had always been recognized as the leader of the Beatles. It was he who had started the band, later bringing in Paul, who found George. When things were going badly, one of the boys would ask him, "Where are we going, Johnny?" His response would be, "To the toppermost of the poppermost!" He was also the oldest of the guitarists, had married first, and had a child. Besides that, John had a sense of bravado, whether onstage or in press conferences, that made his bandmates fall into line behind him. His leadership was about to be sorely tested.

The Beatles left London on August 11 for America, bound for Boston, where they were met by 600 supportive fans. They took a connecting flight to Chicago, where the first concert of the tour would be held. Once they settled into their suite at the Astor Tower Hotel, it was time for a team meeting before their scheduled press conference.

To this point, the leader of the Beatles had refused to back off his statements that he'd made to Maureen Cleave months before. He felt that he was simply being honest, and that he was correct in his views. However, it was clear that the stakes had been raised, and that a misstep in the upcoming press conference could lead to cancellation of the tour. Both Brian Epstein and press secretary Tony Barrow emphasized that this was no joke, and the Beatles' usual flippancy would be inappropriate. They also mentioned that death threats had come in on the heels of the announced Beatle bans in the South.

It was all up to Lennon now, and his bandmates, who always supported him, waited for his response. Feeling the weight of the entire tour on his shoulders, the usually unflappable Beatle burst into tears. He said he didn't mean to put everyone through this and would do whatever it took to make things right. Once he composed himself, the Beatles marched off to meet the press, dressed in somber suits and ties.

Lennon sat at a table, a microphone before him, his bandmates standing behind him. He could not have looked more uncomfortable. Predictably, the first question was a request to clarify the *Datebook* remarks.

"If I'd have said, 'television is more popular than Jesus', I might have got away with it," he began. "I'm sorry I opened my mouth. I just happened to be talking to a friend (Maureen Cleave) and I used the word 'Beatles' as a remote thing—'Beatles' like other people see us. I said they are having more influence on kids and things than anything else, including Jesus. I said it in that way, which was the wrong way. I'm not anti-God, anti-Christ, or anti-religion. I was not knocking it. I was not saying we are greater or better…"

When asked about teenagers who professed that they did, indeed, like the Beatles more than Jesus Christ, he responded, "Well, originally I pointed out that fact in reference to England. That we meant more to kids than Jesus did, or religion at that time. I wasn't knocking it or putting it down… I was just saying it as a fact. It is true, especially more for England than here. I'm not saying that we're better, or greater, or comparing us with Jesus Christ as a person or God as a thing, or whatever it is. I just said what I said and it was wrong. And now it's all this."

Nevertheless, the media still weren't satisfied. Someone asked, "But are you prepared to apologize?"

Lennon, now agitated, tried again: "I wasn't saying what they're saying I was saying," he explained. "I'm sorry I said it—really. I never meant it to be a lousy anti-religious thing. I apologize, if that will make you happy. I still don't know quite what I've done. I've tried to tell you what I did do, but if you want me to apologize, if that will make you happy, then okay, I'm sorry."

Then, to the relief of all, the subject turned to the Beatles' music and the obvious shift in style from lighthearted tunes like "I Want to Hold Your Hand" to the more serious songs, such as "Eleanor Rigby." Here Paul jumped in, taking the pressure off his best friend, and explaining their exploration of new styles, themes, and recording techniques while helping to reduce the tension which had permeated the room at the beginning of the press conference.

This first hurdle cleared, the boys were faced with another interrogation the next day, this time from deejays and journalists covering the tour. Again, Lennon was asked to expound on his views on religion. He stated that he and his bandmates had been forced to grow up very quickly over the past couple years, and that their inquisitive nature had led them to explore beliefs outside of the organized religion they had grown up with as children. And though he did admit to a belief in God, it was "… not as one thing, not as an old man in the sky. I believe what people call God is something in all of us."

Finally, when asked if he felt the Beatles were slipping in popularity due to the religious controversy and changes in their music style, Lennon, as well as the others, said he didn't believe there had been a drop-off, and that this tour would be an indicator.

Thus, the stage was set for the commencement of the North American tour, at the International Amphitheatre in Chicago. Fortunately for the Beatles, the first seven sites of the tour would be in northern US cities, as well as Toronto, Canada. The belief—and hope—of the Beatles and their handlers was that by the time they ventured below the Mason-Dixon line, the furor John Lennon had created would have blown over. Only time would tell.

Chapter Twenty-One

During the week, Marnie kept track of updates on the Beatles situation through TV news, both local and national, and Myles's scouring of the country's major tabloids while at work. And the news was not promising.

In Pennsylvania, for example, a state senator announced he would propose a resolution in the Pennsylvania legislature calling on all talent agents in the state to refuse to book the Beatles and to cancel any bookings already made—most notably, the one at John F. Kennedy Stadium on August 16. He also urged radio and TV stations in the state to stop playing Beatles records, and that owners of juke boxes remove Beatles 45s from their machines. He said, "We can all get along very well without the Beatles, but there are multitudes who cannot get along without Jesus Christ."

And in Boston, a state representative drafted a petition to be offered in the Massachusetts House of Representatives for the city of Boston to revoke the Beatles' permit for their show scheduled at Suffolk Downs horse racing track on August 18, asking, "Who are these creeps before the High and Mighty?"

Meanwhile, across the South, Beatle burnings

began in earnest, with the highlight an Associated Press photo showing the Grand Dragon of the Ku Klux Klan tossing Beatles records onto a fire at the base of a burning cross. And although Marnie's radio station of choice, WHBQ, had not participated in a ban of Beatles records as of yet, she was afraid the shoe would drop any day. It didn't help that she had to listen to Tillie sermonize on the evils that Lennon's remarks had entailed, comparing him to her now-beloved Elvis, who "addresses his elders as 'yes, ma'am' and 'yes, sir' and "praises the Lord in his religious songs."

By the time the weekend rolled around, Marnie had seen the news clips of the Beatles' press conference in Chicago and thought that Lennon looked terrified. She couldn't help but feel sorry for the man, and in general the whole group, who had brought so much joy to so many through their gift of music because she knew this apology would not satisfy their hard-core detractors, especially in the South. It made her angry. She also had a sneaking suspicion that Reverend Hollis was not above putting in his two cents on the issue, capitalizing on the anti-Beatle frenzy that was sweeping through the South. For the first time in a long time she actually considered begging off from Sunday services with her father, claiming a case of "the monthlies," which he would surely not dispute. But then, she reasoned, she'd be just as cowardly as those people piling on the Beatles when they were down. It was time to face the music, so to speak.

And so, with great trepidation she slipped on a yellow sundress and met her father downstairs. As usual, Roy was in a shirt and tie for church, despite the intense heat. But it seemed that something else was making him uncomfortable. She knew that he knew about the whole Beatle mess—how could he not? But as of yet, he hadn't broached the subject with her. Again, she was happy he was working nights and that their overlap at home was at a minimum. Yesterday she had purposely made herself scarce, playing pickup softball with the local boys (even having foregone her Saturday morning Beatles cartoons) down at the neighborhood park rather than hang around the house where he could corner her. Now, as she climbed into the Fairlane, there was nowhere to hide.

They were pulling out the driveway when he said, "Aren't you going to turn on the radio?"

"Sure," she said, clicking on the knob. Thankfully, it was tuned to his favorite country music station. She was never so happy to hear the voices of Buck Owens and his Buckaroos. They rode in silence for a few minutes and were almost to the church when he said, "I think you and I have something to discuss later."

"Okay, Daddy," she replied, a knot forming in her stomach.

The church was pretty full on this sweltering day, with large fans on pedestals positioned in every quarter of the sanctuary blowing air into the congregation, many of whom were fanning themselves with their hymnals. Marnie and her father walked down the middle aisle to the third row from the front, Roy's usual place of preference, and directly in line with the pulpit from which Reverend Hollis would deliver his sermon. They passed Charlotte and her parents, with Mrs. Perkins, her beehive hairdo looking a bit wilted in the heat, offering a weak wave. On the other side, Betty Lou Majors and her cronies sat close by each other, some with their parents.

They had barely reached their seat on the padded wooden pew when the choir began to sing the first hymn and everyone rose to join in. Marnie wasn't much of a singer, but Roy had a rich baritone that he didn't mind showing off, and he got right into it. This was followed by some opening prayers from one of the deacons, another hymn, and then a reading from the Bible by Reverend Hollis.

Marnie knew something was up when the passage Hollis had chosen discussed the sin of worshiping false idols. Indeed, the minister, his craggy face gleaming with sweat beneath that shock of silvery hair, seemed possessed by a fervor that was over the top, even for him. Then, his passage finished, he closed the Bible and fixed his audience with a glowering stare as he paused for effect.

"The Bible tells us," he began calmly, "that it is a sin to indulge in idolatry."

"Amen!" cried someone in the crowd.

"And yet, are not many of us guilty of this very offense? The worship of false gods has no place in the house of the Lord."

"Amen!"

"I have been reminded of these words every day for the past week as I have read the newspaper and watched my television. Who amongst us has heard of the blasphemous statements by this John Lennon of the Beatles?"

Marnie felt the swoosh of hands shooting up throughout the room. Her father hesitated, then raised his as well.

"For those of you who are unaware, allow me to enlighten you. This… *entertainer*, who for some reason has become an idol to millions of young people in our great nation, had the temerity, the absolute *gall*, to claim that he and his fellow Beatles, a bunch of long-haired, effeminate troublemakers, are greater than our Savior, Jesus Christ!"

Someone shouted, "No!"

"Oh, yes, my friends," said Hollis, his voice rising with each sentence. "This Lennon, this *false idol*, is brainwashing our impressionable youth with hidden messages in his songs, leading them towards a life of sin and damnation!"

A few more cried out. Marnie could feel her hands balling into fists on her lap.

"There are even those here amongst us at this very moment who have fallen under his spell!" He fixed Marnie with a stare that was borderline frightening. "It is up to us, as God-fearing, Christian Americans, to reject these false idols and bring those among us who have strayed into line, before they are damned to the flames of hell!"

That tore it for Marnie. On wobbly legs, she rose to her feet and faced the pulpit. There was an audible gasp from the members of the congregation. Even her father looked up at her in shock. "Is it *me* you are referring to, Reverend Hollis?" she called to him in a voice so strong it surprised her. "Because I don't appreciate being singled out, especially when you are dead wrong on this."

Another gasp. Marnie was sure her father was going to yank her down into her seat, but he seemed frozen. So, she locked her knees and grabbed the backrest of the pew in front of her for support, her gaze never leaving the venerable pastor.

If Hollis was taken back by this show of impudence, he didn't reveal it. In fact, he smiled, knowing this callow youngster had given him the perfect opportunity to prove his point. "What is your name, child?" he said patronizingly.

"You know who I am, Reverend," she answered. "Marnie Culpeper. I've been coming to this church all my life. I believe in God, and that Jesus Christ is my Lord and Savior. But I also believe in understanding and compassion for others, and I'm not seeing it in your sermon today."

The crowd broke out into a loud murmur, and someone dramatically bleated, "Cast her out!"

Like Moses in the desert, Hollis raised his hands to quell the uprising. "No," he said sternly, "let the child speak." Silence fell over the assemblage. "Now then, could you please explain to us how the blasphemous remarks of this man, who makes his living shaking his long hair on stage while delusional teenaged girls swoon at his feet, can be interpreted in any other way than what he stated? A proclamation that he is, indeed, more important that Jesus Christ?"

Standing her ground, Marnie fired back: "He did *not* say that he, or the Beatles for that matter, are more important than Jesus. What he *did* say was that in these modern times, it seems that young people are looking in other directions besides religion for answers."

"Answers to *what*?" he boomed at the ceiling.

"Answers to why thousands of people go hungry in the richest country in the world. Why we put down people whose skin color or religion is different from ours. Why we feel it necessary to drop bombs on strangers in other countries who haven't done us any harm. Don't *you* worry about these things, Reverend? Because *I* sure do."

Now the stunned congregation looked to their leader for his response. The man seemed surprised this young girl was standing up to him and conducting herself quite well at that. "Of course I worry about these things, child," he said. "And that is why, in these times of turmoil, we need the guidance of our Savior, Jesus Christ, more than ever before. We cannot, and *will* not, let ourselves be diverted from our divine cause by some loudmouthed atheist!"

"Amen!" called out more than a few parishioners.

Marnie knew she had lost. "All right, then, Reverend," she said, biting off each word. "If that's the way you see it, fine. You won't change your mind, and neither will I. So, I guess you're right. I'm beyond salvation, and my place is not here." With that, she brushed past her father, who could not react in time to grab her, made it to the end of the pew, then turned down the aisle and walked with measured steps towards the rear of the church, her eyes focused straight ahead, willing herself not to trip, trying not to acknowledge the reactions of the parishioners, ranging from shaking heads to hands held over mouths (especially Betty Lou and her friends) to the steely-eyed disgust from Charlotte's parents and those around them. After what seemed like a hundred yards she exited the church into the blinding sunlight, descended the front steps, and began the long walk home.

* * *

An agonizing hour later, Roy entered the house, slamming the door behind him. As he climbed the stairs to her room, Marnie tried to remember the last time she'd been paddled for misbehaving and braced herself for the worst.

But her father surprised her. In a barely controlled voice he said, while standing over her, "Do you have any idea what you've gone and done?"

"Yes, sir," she said, eyes downcast.

"No, I don't think you do," he countered. "First of all, I had to suffer the embarrassment of that whole congregation eyeballing me for the rest of the service. Then, no sooner than I got outside, I had Reverend Hollis lecturing me about how I was incapable of raising my child properly, how I've allowed you to run wild and disrespect your elders and the church. Then, when he was done with me, I had all these people, some of whom I don't even know, telling me how sorry they were for me, and that they were going to pray for me, and for you, and for your salvation. It was just horrible."

He paused and took a deep breath. "Then, when I thought it couldn't get any worse, here comes Sam Perkins with his wife and daughter in tow, to tell me that 'your services will no longer be needed' at Perkins' Market. He said your presence might cause a commotion, what with people gawking at you and such, and it might also give the impression his family condones your behavior."

Marnie was thunderstruck. "How dare that man look down on me!" she wailed. "After the way he treated Tillie's son, he's trying to make like he's the model of Christian behavior? I don't believe this!"

"Well, you'd better," he replied. "And mark my words, little girl, this is just the beginning of what you brought down on our heads. What on earth made you think you could backtalk a man of God in front of all those people? Is that the way I've raised you?"

"No, sir," she mumbled.

"Well, it's clear to me now that somewhere things have gone off the rails," he concluded. "And I have to feel that all this—" he swept his arm across the room at the Beatles-covered walls "—sure hasn't been helping. In fact, I think you're taking after this guy, thinking you can say whatever you want, to whoever you want, whenever you feel like it."

"But Daddy—"

"Don't backtalk me!" he exploded. "It's clear I've lost control of you, so we're gonna start correcting this right here and now. You are grounded until further notice, and that includes the concert. You call your friend Myles and tell him you will *not* be attending. Do you read me?"

Marnie had never seen her father so angry. To dispute him would have been suicidal. "Yes, sir," she said, trying not to cry, as he turned on his heel and stalked out of the room, slamming her door behind him so violently that a handful of Beatles photos fluttered from the walls to the floor.

Chapter Twenty-Two

Because the Beatles pretty much performed a half hour concert set of ten to eleven songs, there was the necessity for a number of preliminary acts to not only get the crowd warmed up but give the attendees the impression they were getting a real value for the price of admission. The lineup changed with each year and tour, but the North American dates of 1966 included R&B singer Bobby Hebb, East Coast girl group the Ronettes, a Boston-based group called the Remains, and a Brian Epstein-managed band, the Cyrcle.

The Beatles, hoping their press conferences and John's mea culpa had diffused the volatile situation in America, kicked off the tour with two shows (3:00 PM and 7:00 PM) at Chicago's International Amphitheatre on August 12. For each show the arena was near its capacity of 13,000. As for their set list, it was a mixture of tunes from the 1963-1965 era, including covers of Chuck Berry's "Rock and Roll Music" and Little Richard's "Long Tall Sally" to open and close the shows. Those preferring Lennon-McCartney compositions could enjoy "She's a Woman," "Day Tripper," "Baby's in Black," "I Feel Fine," "Yesterday," "Nowhere Man," and "Paperback Writer," while George and Ringo chipped in with "If I

Needed Someone" and "I Wanna be Your Man" respectively.

As was the norm in previous concert tours, the hordes of teens in the Amphitheatre screamed their heads off from start to finish, and local reviews observed that in Chicago, anyway, the Beatles' transgressions seemed to have been forgiven.

The band carried on to Detroit for another double-concert date on August 13, and the total attendance of 28,000, a near sellout at Olympia Stadium, was again encouraging, despite some anti-Lennon picketers outside the arena.

So far, the Midwest had been very positive for the Beatles, but on the same day as they performed before hysterically cheering fans in Chicago, radio station KLUE-AM in Longview, Texas, had held a Beatles bonfire. According to the Associated Press, the event had been attended by hundreds of youths, who either actively participated in or witnessed the burning.

On the day of Marnie Culpeper's outburst during church services in Memphis, the Beatles were to perform an evening concert at Cleveland's cavernous Municipal Stadium. This event, however, produced an interesting subplot of foreboding. On the morning of this Sunday, during services at Cleveland's New Haven Baptist church, Pastor Thurman H. Babbs warned his parishioners that those who attended the Beatles concert that evening would be expelled from the congregation, and that the time had come for Christians to stand up and speak out against the Beatles.

It was not noted how many concertgoers from Reverend Babbs's parishioners boycotted the concert; however, the 20,000 fans who did show up were, to say the least, enthusiastic, with a few thousand breaking through a restraining fence around the stage during "Day Tripper." The security police were simply overwhelmed and unable to contain the surge, causing the concert to be halted for a half hour or so until order could be restored.

Then it was on to Washington, D.C., the southernmost venue of the tour so far, for an evening concert at D.C. Stadium. In a pre-concert press conference that convened in the baseball locker room of the Washington Senators ballclub, one reporter suggested that the Beatles were actually using the remarks made by John Lennon as a publicity stunt to boost sluggish ticket sales. The Beatles' leader, barely controlling his anger, dismissed such cynical reasoning as stupid, saying that the group did not want that kind of negative publicity.

Lennon had also been interviewed prior to the concert date by the *Washington Post,* and the subsequent article was sympathetic to his predicament, detailing his experiences with organized religion from childhood onward, and portraying him as a young man groping for answers in both his personal life and his music. When asked for his reaction to the Beatle bonfires, he said, "That was a real shock, the physical burning. I couldn't go away knowing that I created another little piece of hate in the world. Especially with something as uncomplicated as people listening to a record and dancing and enjoying what the Beatles are. Not when I could do something about it. If I said tomorrow I'm not going to play again, I still couldn't live in a place with somebody hating me for something irrational… But that's the trouble with being truthful."

To their relief, the D.C. Stadium concert went smoothly, despite the presence of a handful of the Prince George's County Ku Klux Klan, dressed in red, white and green robes, and led by the Imperial Wizard of the Maryland chapter, who picketed outside the ballpark while the group performed before over 32,000 screaming fans.

The North American tour was now one third complete, but one date loomed ominously on the horizon: the 19th of August in Memphis, Tennessee.

Chapter Twenty-Three

The late afternoon of Tuesday, August 16th, found Marnie alone at home, her father having left for work. Since her emotionally charged grounding two days previously, the two had kept out of each other's way and there was a sense of relief when she was alone, even if the extent of her evening entailed a dinner of heated up beanie weenies and watching *The Girl From U.N.C.L.E.*, her favorite TV spy show. She was listening to the *Help!* album and sticking red colored pins into her 1966 Beatles tour map of North America when the phone rang. Happy to have any contact whatsoever with the outside world, she ran downstairs and eagerly picked up.

"How's it going?" asked Myles, who had listened sympathetically to her blow-by-blow account of Sunday's drama via a previous telephone conversation.

"Just great. I'm about to rearrange my magazine collection for the zillionth time. Then it's an exciting dinner of beanie weenies and cornbread."

"Yum."

"So, what's up?"

"Well," he said, "since your dad's on night shift, what would you say to a little entertainment this evening?"

"What did you have in mind?"

"How about a Beatle burning?"

"*What?*"

"Here's the deal, Marnie. As you know, one of my illustrious jobs at work is bringing everyone's mail upstairs. Well, we've got this one guy in the mailroom, a real goober, who was bragging to one of the females that tonight there's going to be a big old Beatles bonfire just outside of town."

"Wow," she said. "I'm surprised I didn't hear about it on the radio. But then again, these burnings are happening everywhere in the South, so why not here? There's just one problem, Myles. Even if I wanted to go and run the risk of my dad finding out and killing me, how would we even get there?"

"You seem to forget that I've recently acquired my learner's permit," he answered suavely, "and I pretty much have the driving thing down already. Besides, my mom's car is an automatic that a monkey could drive."

"And your parents would actually let you go?"

"Not exactly. See, my dad is away on business in Minnesota and my mom is, right now, at a Garden Club meeting, which is just a weak excuse for her and her friends to gossip and get sloshed. If she holds true to form, I'd say that by seven she's out cold till tomorrow morning. So, are you game?"

"I don't know. Do you even know how to get to this place?"

"I heard the guy mention a location—a patch of abandoned farmland about a half hour drive from here—so I got hold of a map and found it."

"And you think we'd be back before midnight?"

"Way before. C'mon, you know you want to go. We wouldn't get involved, of course. Just kind of check it out. And if it gets out of hand, we'll just leave. Hey, who knows, maybe you'll even see someone you know?"

"Yeah, like Betty Lou, or even Charlotte," she said in disgust. "Okay, then, count me in."

"Groovy. I'll see you around eight. And Marnie, don't do anything crazy like wear one of your Beatles tee shirts. We want to low-key this."

"Gotcha." She hung up the phone, her body tingling, and forced herself to eat some dinner so she wouldn't be starving later on. Then, after washing the dishes she dashed upstairs to pick out some inconspicuous dark clothing, feeling very *Girl From U.N.C.L.E.*-ish.

True to his word, Myles pulled up in front of the Culpeper residence at 7:45 PM in his mother's navy-blue Plymouth Valiant, a fairly nondescript two-door hardtop. Marnie scurried outside and hopped in. Her friend was dressed similarly, with a dark baseball cap completing his stealthy ensemble. "Okay, here's the directions to the place," he said, handing her a piece of paper. "You're the navigator."

"Roger."

Myles eased onto the gas pedal but the car didn't move. "Don't you have to put it in DRIVE first?" she asked suspiciously.

"Oops, sorry," he replied. "Just a little excited."

"Uh-huh."

They cruised along slowly, staying under the speed limit and coming to full stops at every traffic light and stop sign. A police stop would prove disastrous. "This is kind of a cruddy car," Marnie said, noticing a distinct rattle underneath every time he accelerated.

"It's my mom's around-town-mobile," he explained. "Perfect for our little outing. I don't think we'd want to be pulling up to this event in my dad's red Eldorado."

"Good point."

Soon they were approaching the Memphis city limits. "One thing's bothering me, Myles," Marnie said. "All the bonfires I've read about have been these highly publicized to-dos held in public parking lots and such. Why is this one so out of the way?"

"Guess we'll just have to find out," he said with a shrug.

It had gone completely dark by the time they made their approach to the site. "Look for a lot of cars," Myles suggested. They drove around a little on some back roads, with no luck. Then, in the distance Marnie saw a sizable group of vehicles on the edge of the field. Beyond them were people, but no tell-tale bonfire flames.

Marnie peered through the windshield. "Myles, stop the car," she said suddenly.

He rolled to a halt and put the car in PARK on the side of the dirt road. "What's the matter?"

"When the moon came out from behind the clouds I could've sworn I saw a big cross in that field beyond the cars."

"You mean—"

"I can't be sure, but this is no ordinary bonfire, buddy."

"What do you want to do?"

Marnie thought quickly. "Turn off your headlights and pull into those woods near the road," she said, pointing, and he did so. "Kill the engine," she then commanded. It was dead quiet all around them, save for a few crickets.

Myles was clearly nervous. All the cool nonchalance he'd exhibited earlier seemed to have drained from his body. "What now?" he said shakily.

"Well," she answered, "we've got two choices. We can just turn tail and go home, or we can sneak over to those cars and see what-all's going on. I'm willing to do it if you are."

Now Myles was the doubtful one. "Jeez, I don't know—" he began.

"Hey, you're the one that dragged me out here," she snapped with annoyance. "You want to back out now?"

"No, it's not that, I just, uh …" he spluttered.

"Why don't we do this, then? I'll go check it out. You wait here for me."

Embarrassed, he said, "No, I can't let you go alone. Let's do it."

"Figured you'd say that," she said with a smile. "We'll sneak up to those cars—they're about a hundred yards away—and see what's what. Just stay low. You're a lot taller than me. And try not to trip in the dark, okay?"

"Yeah."

They crept, hunched over, across the rutted, cracked field that had once produced cotton or tobacco. After what seemed like miles, they'd reached the vehicles. Most were pickup trucks, some with gun racks in their cabs or flatbeds. Confederate flag decals adorned many of their bumpers or windows. When the teens looked to the center of the field they spied a huge wooden cross and a group of hooded figures in white robes being called to order.

"Oh, crap, it's the Klan," said Marnie.

It was common knowledge that the Ku Klux Klan had chapters in and around Memphis. In fact, Tennessee had played a key role in its formation in the days of Reconstruction that followed the Civil War. Its founder, Confederate cavalry general Nathan Bedford Forrest, even had a memorial statue in a Memphis public park that bore his name. The fact that two other major parks in town were named "Confederate" and "Jefferson Davis" did little to dispel the idea that the Klan—and all they represented as an organization of hatred and terrorism for non-whites and non-Christians—was alive and well in the area. However, in Marnie's lifetime they had seemed to exist only in the shadows, and she was fascinated to finally see them in the flesh.

Myles, on the other hand, was petrified. It was no secret that Jews were pretty high on the "hated" list for the Klan. He looked like he wanted to dig a hole in this rock-hard field and crawl into it. "Marnie," he whispered, "could we leave, please?"

"Sshh," she said, swatting a mosquito on her forearm. "Let's give it five minutes. I want to see what they're up to. Looks like they're starting. Man, they must be sweatin' bullets in those outfits."

Indeed, each of the fifty-plus Klansmen was attired in the traditional regalia of the order: a flowing white ankle-length robe with long sleeves that featured a circular red patch on the chest, inlaid with a white and black cross-like symbol. Their faces were obscured by a conical white hood with a front and back flap through which eyeholes had been cut. The men—at least it seemed like all were men—were each holding a long pole of some type. These turned out to be torches, their ends previously wrapped with burlap and soaked in gasoline. A Klansman was going around with a cigarette lighter, setting the torches aflame.

In the flickering of the torches Marnie could see the twenty-foot tall wooden cross with more definition, its crosspiece lashed into place with heavy rope. There were, indeed, Beatle albums and other paraphernalia laid at its base, and a single LP record had been nailed to the crosspiece intersection.

"Circle the cross!" commanded one of the Klansmen, who sported a more ornate outfit that included a cape with red trim. The participants fanned out to where they stood a few feet apart, facing inward, torches blazing. "Klansmen, light the cross!" was the next command. They moved as one towards the wooden cross and touched their torches to the Beatles materials at the base. Immediately the pile caught fire, and the flame snaked its way up the structure and out on the crosspiece. The vinyl LP began to melt and drip.

"Do you accept the light?" called the leader.

"Yes!" the Klansmen yelled in unison.

"Then repeat after me:

For my God!

For my race!

For my Klan!

For my nation!"

The Klansmen chanted as one, their still-flaming torches held aloft.

"Behold the fiery cross!" cried the leader. "Still brilliant! All the troubled history has failed to quench its hallowed flames!" He paused for effect as the cross crackled behind him. "We are here tonight, my brothers, to recognize a threat that has been made to our existence, the very core of our beliefs. You are aware that this God-hating atheist Lennon and his band of Communist subversives are coming to the very heart of our home next week to spread their disgusting love of vile black music, and their disease of non-belief in the sanctity of our Lord Jesus Christ?"

"Yes!" cried the circled figures.

"Then I say to you here and now, that as God-fearing white Americans it is our sworn duty to stop them in their tracks!"

"Yes!"

"Make no mistake, my brothers, we are at war, a war in which the hearts and minds of our youth are at stake. And so, like our forefathers a century ago, it is up to us to rise up against those who would threaten our way of life and smite them as God struck down his enemies in biblical times!" He paused and lifted the face flap of his headdress to spit what looked to be a large stream of tobacco juice. Marnie blanched at the sight. Then he leaned over and picked off the ground a hunting rifle with a telescopic sight, holding it aloft as the Klansmen howled with glee. "On Friday night, August 19th, 1966, we will strike a decisive blow in our fight against the forces of evil!" he bellowed. "Are you with me?"

"*Yes!*"

Marnie had seen enough. "Wanna get out of here?" she hissed.

"I thought you'd never ask."

They ran, doubled over, all the way back to the stand of trees where the Valiant lay hidden, and jumped in. "Don't patch out or anything," cautioned Marnie. "Easy does it. And leave your lights off for a few minutes."

"If my hand would stop shaking, I could turn the damn ignition on," he replied, the keys jingling between his bony fingers. After a few attempts they finally got underway and rode in silence until they reached the city limits. It was only then that Myles spoke up. "I hate those guys," he said, attempting a weak joke.

But instead of a laugh, he was shocked to hear Marnie break out in sobs. The boy had never seen her cry before and was totally confused as to how he should react. He gripped the steering wheel tightly and managed a halting, "H-hey, you okay there?"

"No, I'm *not* okay," she said between jagged breaths. "Myles, I saw something frightening back there."

"We both did."

"No, something else. When the guy in charge, the one waving the rifle around, lifted his mask, I could see he has this big birthmark on the side of his face."

"So?"

She turned to him, her face awash with tears. "And so does my daddy's boss."

"Wait… you think it's the same guy? A *policeman?*"

"It has to be. I mean, what are the odds? And there have always been rumors about Lieutenant Sutter and the Klan."

"But aren't the police gonna be in charge of *protecting* the Beatles in Memphis?"

"You tell me, because from what I just heard, the Klan wants them dead."

Myles swallowed hard. "So, what are we going to do, Marnie?"

"I don't know," she whispered.

Chapter Twenty-Four

As the Beatles flew to Philadelphia for their August 16th evening concert, they couldn't help but notice the newspaper articles about their tour and the religious controversy swirling around it were sharing space with news reports on the Vietnam War and racial strife in America. The *Miami News*, for example, featured a photo of two screaming female concert fans underneath the headline "**26 S. Viet Citizens Die—U.S. Jet Plows into Village.**" The *Desert Sun* of Palm Springs, California displayed headlines entitled "**Fans Hail Beatles in Chicago**" and "**700 Negroes March in Chicago**" side-by-side. More ominously, the *Victoria Advocate* in Texas featured a photo of a Beatles bonfire nearby to the headline "**Chicago Rioting Continues as Police Battle in Park.**"

The Philadelphia date at John F. Kennedy Stadium went off well, though the crowd of 20,000 was only a third of the facility's capacity. Then it was on to Toronto, Canada, for two shows at the Maple Leaf Gardens hockey arena on the 17th, the total attendance estimated at around 32,000.

During a press conference between the Toronto shows, the Beatles were asked their opinion on the increase in young American men, labeled "draft dodgers," moving north of the border into Canada rather than serve in the American military. Interestingly, George Harrison defended their right not to serve in the Vietnam War by citing the Seventh Commandment, "Thou Shalt Not kill." Of course, the Christianity issue came up, and both Harrison and John Lennon commented that although there was much that was right with it, some of its basic concepts were not being followed. Editorials in Canada tended to be more supportive of Lennon's remarks than in America.

The Beatles then pushed on to Boston and Suffolk Downs racetrack, where they performed before some 25,000 fans, including members of the Kennedy family, who had driven up from the family compound at Hyannis Port.

It was during these last few days of touring in the North that a British journalist who was working on a documentary about the tour sat down for an interview with Robert Shelton, the Imperial Wizard of the Ku Klux Klan. Well-dressed in a conservative suit and tie, Shelton spoke freely on his views of the Beatles and what they represented, as well as his thoughts on the Beatles' upcoming visit to Memphis:

"...the basic belief and philosophy of the Klan is to uphold the concept of Christianity, and it is certainly distasteful, since this is the Bible Belt of the nation, particularly in the southern part of America, to have Parliament in England ban myself from visiting, when at the same time these individuals who want to vilify Christ can come to America and still continue to collect sums of money. I think this is a dangerous trend..." He then went on to compare the Beatles' values with those of a socialist or communist regime.

When asked about the Klan taking issue with Lennon's remarks about Christianity, and whether the Beatles' views on civil rights and color were more annoying, Shelton replied, "It's hard to tell through the mop heads whether they're white or black.... I don't have any knowledge of their involvement in civil rights. The only attitude I can assume is that they're interested in one thing, and that's the greenback dollar... If it would be more popular for them to be black, I'm sure they'd consider themselves black; if it's popular to be white, they'd be white. All they're after is the fast buck."

* * *

As early as August 10th, the mayor of Memphis and the Board of Commissioners, referring to Memphis as "a city of churches," had issued a unanimous resolution to express "official disapproval" of the Beatles' August 19th concert date at the Mid-South Coliseum and "advise the Beatles they are not welcome in the city of Memphis." Regardless of this proclamation, the concert was not canceled.

The space-age shaped Mid-South Coliseum, a domed facility seating 10,085 people, had been erected in 1963 on Early Maxwell Boulevard in Memphis. By the summer of 1965 it had become the premier concert performance center in the city and had promoted various African American acts including the Drifters, Muddy Waters, and Stevie Wonder. Equally significant was the integration of the adjacent fairgrounds and public recreational facilities, including the fairgrounds' public pool.

The Mid-South Coliseum continued its evolution into a major venue for rock and roll concerts, with promoter/TV personality Dick Clark becoming involved. Thus, began a parade of mid-60s acts including Peter and Gordon, Herman's Hermits, the Dave Clark Five, and the Rolling Stones, who represented the "British Invasion" of America begun by the Beatles in 1964.

The Memphis media reported on the rock and roll concerts with more interest than the "soul music" events, primarily because their reader base was predominantly white. Also, the rockers tended to be more flamboyant and elicit more dramatic reaction from the teen crowds. For example, in the Memphis *Commercial Appeal*, columnist Larry Williams wrote that a performance by Herman's Hermits, a rather vanilla British group that mirrored the Beatles' 1963 "mop top" persona, caused "an H-bomb of destruction in the form of long hair, wiggly hips, and shrill, screechy noise…its practitioners are invariably young, energetic, loud, brassy, and untalented." This form of music was considered a weak imitation of the style popularized by native son Elvis Presley.

And while *Commercial Appeal*'s columnist Connie Richards felt the Coliseum had "added a new element to our entertainment fun," the very manager of the venue, Jim Ohust, discussed a Rolling Stones concert by saying "by the time they came on, the audience is hysterical. The kids spit, holler and curse. In the fury of trying to get backstage they weep, throw things, stand on chairs and scream. They come in nice kids and they leave nice kids, but for that half hour, it's something. Cortez must have used something like this during the height of the Mayan Sun Rallies. Little girls, who probably never express affection to their own parents, scream 'I love you!' over and over at the top of their lungs." And though Ohust had much to gain financially by booking these acts, he was convinced that this type of rock and roll was just a fad, saying, "Some of these longhairs don't even belong in the world of entertainment. They're ill-attired, they're surly, and have no manners…unless you're in the first few rows, you can't hear a thing. You can't see them afterwards to get autographs or take pictures. They're money conscious groups. Herman's Hermits spent about 25 minutes on stage—no autographs, no nothing. That's very little to give when you are making between ten and twenty thousand dollars a night…"

However, the hypercritical Ohust did offer this disclaimer: "The imitators may be dropping by the wayside, but the Beatles, who started it all, are still thriving. Maybe that's because they still have the personality that established them in the first place, and also because they have brains under those mops of hair."

Thus, the stage was set for the Beatles to make their first appearance in Memphis, with shows at 4 PM and 8:30 PM that would send their local supporters into delirium and set the cash registers to singing.

Chapter Twenty-Five

On the morning of Wednesday, August 17th, Marnie and Myles, who had ridden over on his black English racer 3-speed bicycle, sat on the Culpepers' front steps, sipping lemonade Tillie had prepared from scratch. The boy, exhausted from the ride in that day's draining humidity, savored the tart liquid as it slid down his throat, then pressed the icy glass to his forehead. "Have you thought about what we saw last night?" he asked.

"Are you kidding? I never even got to sleep," she responded. "All I've been doing is thinking about it. I just don't know what to *do* about it."

"Yeah," he said. "I couldn't sleep, either; that's why I called in sick today, which I'm sure my dad won't approve of when he finds out." He took a sip. "This really puts you in a tough spot, Marnie. It's not like you can say, 'Hey, Daddy, the other night I just happened to be at this KKK cross burning and—'"

"Exactly. I'd never get any farther 'cause he'd go wild."

As if on cue, Roy appeared at the side of the house. "I'm heading to the hardware store," he said. "We need some light bulbs." He began to walk towards the garage, then stopped and turned back.

"Myles, you are aware that Marnie won't be attending the concert Friday night, aren't you?"

"Yessir."

"Okay, then. Maybe you can find someone else to take the ticket."

After he pulled out of the driveway, Myles chuckled ruefully. "Well, no change of heart there."

"Nope."

"So, back to the problem. How do we stop this thing from happening on Friday?"

"I've got an idea," she said. "Why don't we try calling the newspaper?"

"The *Commercial Appeal*?"

"Yeah. Like an anonymous tip."

"That could work," he said.

"But we'll have to do it from a pay phone, or else they might be able to trace the call, like they do on TV."

"That means *I'll* have to do it, because in case you haven't noticed, you're grounded."

"Uh-huh. Well, there's a pay phone near the gas station a couple blocks from here. Have you got some pocket change?"

"Yeah. Now how exactly should I word this?"

"Well, I wouldn't say anything about a policeman being involved. Heck, I don't even know if y'all should mention the KKK. I mean, who knows if there's any Klan guys working at the newspaper?"

"Really? You think that's possible?"

"Myles, if there's one or more on the Memphis PD, they could be *anywhere*."

"Good point. I'll just say that I have it on good information that there will be an assassination attempt on the Beatles during the Friday night concert. Sutter, if that's who it was, specified the evening performance, right?"

"That was the way I heard it."

Myles shook his head. "Of course, you realize how crazy this will all sound, right?"

"Yeah, but it's worth a shot."

"No pun intended?"

"Oops, sorry. Well, you go make the call, and I'll wait here for you."

He pedaled off, a determined look on his angular face. She wondered if he would tense up under pressure, or his voice would start cracking over the phone. None of it was encouraging.

When Myles returned around twenty minutes later and flipped down the kickstand to his English racer with some extra force, she knew his mission had been a failure. He dejectedly sank down on the steps next to her and said, "They laughed at me."

"They didn't take it seriously at all?"

"Well, first of all, even though I tried to deepen my voice a little, they knew it was a kid who was calling. Then, whoever it was on the other end told me that there have been death threats phoned in to local newspapers in every city the Beatles have played since the Jesus Christ thing broke. In fact, my call was the third one to the *Commercial Appeal* this week! The other two were by people who were actually threatening to *do* it, religious nuts or whatever."

"So that's all they said?"

"No. The guy said I should contact the Memphis PD directly and talk to the officer who will be in charge of the Beatles' security detail."

"And who's that?"

"Lieutenant Joe Bob Sutter."

Marnie hung her head. "Well, that was a waste of time, but at least you tried, Myles."

"So now what?"

"There's only one option. I'm gonna have to try and clue my father in about what's gonna happen Friday night."

"Good luck with that. I've been wondering, though…you don't think Sutter is going to be the actual trigger man, do you?"

"No, he'd be too smart to get his own hands dirty. But I saw a lot of other rednecks at that rally that would gladly do it. The thing is, Sutter is the one who can *allow* it to happen, and that's what I've somehow got to get across to my father without sounding crazier than he thinks I am already."

"You've only got today and tomorrow. All I can tell you is good luck." He paused, and even managed a wry smile. "By the way, about that ticket… I get the impression you'll be hanging onto it, am I right?"

"Could be," she said. "You haven't told your parents about my grounding, have you?"

"Nope."

"Good."

"So, you're still planning on going?"

"I didn't say that. I just want to leave my options open." She frowned, thinking hard. "Sutter's the key. As the head of the Beatles' security detail he can put the men anywhere he wants, including my father. My guess is that he'll get Daddy out of the way, somehow. Personally, I think Daddy can't stand Sutter, though he probably doesn't realize how truly vile the man is. But that is his commander and he believes in doing things by the book, which means following orders. It's really frustrating."

"Well, keep me posted. We'll figure this out."

"I hope." She watched him as he rode away, becoming smaller and smaller until he topped a rise and disappeared.

Once back inside, Marnie was treated to the last thing she needed, a lecture from Tillie, who was leaning over the sink, peeling potatoes. "I just can't believe you sassed a man of the cloth," she said, with a few tut-tuts thrown in. "Or that you're actually taking up for someone who says he's better than Jesus. Lord have mercy." Rather than get into a debate with the woman, she just mumbled a few "sorrys" and dragged herself upstairs to serve out the rest of the day's sentence, totally worn out from lack of sleep and the weight of her situation. She was sitting on her bed with *Meet the Beatles* playing quietly, wondering how on earth to broach the subject with her father, when he surprised her with a rap on the door.

"Mind if I come in?" he said.

"Not at all, Daddy," she said, quickly turning off the phonograph.

"I just got a call from Reverend Hollis," he began, his eyes crinkling as he scanned her Beatles tour map. "He wanted to extend a personal invitation to you to attend a Christian youth rally that will be held at the North Hall across town. The rally's being run by a Reverend Jimmy Stroud, who's supposed to be a very powerful speaker. It's scheduled for the same time as your British friends are playing over at the Coliseum, and Reverend Hollis said they're expecting upwards of 5,000 people."

"You mean, like an anti-Beatles rally?"

"More like a *pro-Jesus* rally," he answered sharply. "I told him you probably wouldn't be interested, but that if you were I would find someone to run you over there. Maybe the Perkins family will be going."

The thought of having to sit with Charlotte and her Bible-thumping, self-righteous parents turned Marnie's stomach. "I think I'll pass on that, Daddy," she said, trying to hide her distaste. "I don't think I could take Reverend Hollis staring me down, even if he's not going to be the only minister there."

"I figured you'd feel that way," he said with a disappointed sigh and turned to leave.

"Daddy?"

"What?"

"Could I ask you something?"

"Sure, but make it quick, I'm on the job in a half hour."

Marnie took a deep breath and said, "What exactly are the police going to be doing as far as the Beatles, once they get to town?"

"Why is that any concern of yours?"

"Just wonderin'."

"Well," he said, "they're going to need a motorcycle escort from the airport to the Coliseum on Friday morning. Then, I'm sure there's going to be a large security detail for both of the concerts, and more mounted police to get them back to the airport. In fact, we're having a squad meeting about it tomorrow. But again, what does this matter to you?"

She decided to go for it. "What if somebody told you they had information that someone was gonna try to shoot the Beatles during the concert. Would you try to stop it?"

Roy's face flushed red. "How can you even ask me that?" he said. "My sworn duty as a police officer is to uphold the law. It doesn't matter what I personally think about those Beatles—they're in my city, and as such they will be under the protection of Memphis PD. End of story."

"I'm not talking about *you*, Daddy. I know how dedicated you are about your job, and how you always try to be fair. But just supposing there were others on the force that would purposely slack off, look the other way?"

Although his daughter was trying to be vague, Roy felt her implication was clear. "Marnie," he said, "I might not approve of the attitudes or beliefs of some of my colleagues, even those who outrank me, but I have to think that when push comes to shove they will do what's right and maintain law and order."

"But things still happen, Daddy. What about the James Meredith shooting a couple months ago?" Meredith, the first black man to enroll in the University of Mississippi in 1962, had been staging a one-man "March Against Fear" from Memphis to Jackson, Mississippi, which was being followed by a handful of news photographers (but no police escort) when he was confronted and shot by a white man wielding a shotgun near Hernando, Mississippi. Meredith had survived, but the incident had shocked people nationwide because of its blatant disregard for the law and because Southern police, who had built a bad enough reputation during the Civil Rights Movement, were nowhere to be seen.

"The Meredith shooting was out of my jurisdiction," Roy said angrily, "and you can bet that if I see anyone—*anyone*—not doing his job on Friday, he'll have to answer to me. Do you read me?"

"Yes, Daddy."

"Good. Now, I've got to go to work. Don't you go spending your time worrying about me and my men doing our duty. Just worry about yourself, because from where I sit, that seems to be a full-time job."

* * *

Roy drove to headquarters, parked his car and went to the locker room, where he changed into his neatly pressed uniform that Tillie had worked on earlier that morning before packing it. He was adjusting the hat when Joe Bob Sutter poked his head into the locker room. "My office, on the double," he said.

Roy was there in less than a minute. "Yes, Lieutenant?" he said upon entering the room.

"Shut the door, Sergeant," said Sutter, "and have a seat."

Roy did as he was instructed and respectfully removed his hat. It was clear his superior officer was a bit on edge, which was to be expected, considering what they were in for on Friday. "Okay," he began, "so we got these longhairs comin' in here Friday morning, and we've gotta deal with everything that involves. There have been a few incidents at the concerts, like in Cleveland for example, of kids gettin' rowdy and tearing the place up. That's *not* gonna happen here, or heads will roll."

"Yes, sir," said Roy. "Crowd control is definitely a priority. But, ah, have you received any reports about possible death threats to the musicians?"

Sutter seemed taken back. "What, you heard something?"

"No sir," Roy responded calmly, "it's just that, you know, they seem to have ticked off a lot of people down here—"

"That's putting it mildly," Sutter said with a grunt, his anger making the wine stain on his jaw even redder. "No good commie atheists is what they are. But anyway, here's the plan. Tomorrow afternoon we'll need you to come in a little early. I want to have a squad meeting for everybody who will be on the security detail Friday, and we're talking about upwards of a hundred men. We'll have a motorcycle unit at the airport to meet their plane, and an armored vehicle to transport them. Then, once they get to the Coliseum, I want you to head up the detail on the floor of the facility for both concerts. I'm told they've built a stage seven feet off the ground and surrounded it with a five-foot chain-link fence in case any delinquents want to rush the stage. We'll have men positioned inside the fence, at all the exits, and in the aisles."

"What about the upstairs rooms and the catwalks?"

"The upstairs level will be closed off and left vacant. We will station men at the bottom of the access stairways on each end to keep anyone from going upstairs." He paused, and his eyes narrowed a bit. "Unfortunately, I'm gonna have to split my time between the evening concert and this big old religious rally they're staging across town, so whenever I'm not on-site, you become the man in charge. Can you handle it?"

"Yes, sir."

"I'm counting on that. And Sergeant?"

"Yes, sir?"

"Don't screw this up."

Chapter Twenty-Six

The next day Marnie slept late, due in equal parts to her exhaustion and the fact that it was Tillie's day off. When she did awaken, she had some buttered toast for breakfast and then undertook a series of mundane tasks she'd been putting off, including cleaning out her closet, all the while playing her Beatles records.

Then she had an idea. She had recently seen an article in *Seventeen* magazine about this new thing called Transcendental Meditation, which was a way to calm yourself down and think positive thoughts. It seemed pretty easy to her. You had to sit Indian-style and close your eyes, or just focus on something in the distance, and clear your mind by silently reciting something called a mantra—a word or sound that has no meaning—over and over, for about twenty minutes. Since the article said you needed an instructor to give you a mantra, she made up her own, assumed the position with her hands on her knees, and tried to meditate, figuring it might help clear her troubled mind.

Despite this being her first attempt at meditation, Marnie became so focused that she didn't even know, as she sat cross-legged on her bed staring up at the Beatles poster above the headboard with her back to the door, that her father had tried to pop in to say goodbye before he left for work. But the sight of his daughter gently rocking back and forth as if in a trance, while the incredibly weird "Tomorrow Never Knows" droned from her phonograph, had made Roy Culpeper back out of the room, shaking his head in dismay.

* * *

Her father had barely left the driveway when Marnie suddenly snapped out of her self-induced transcendental reverie, a word coming to her like a lightning bolt. "Of course!" she cried aloud. "How could I have not thought of it? I'm so stupid!" She looked at the alarm clock on her nightstand. It was only 11 AM. Plenty of time for her to succeed where Myles had so miserably failed. Hurriedly she threw on a clean tee shirt, jeans and sneakers, followed by a trip to her piggy bank, from which she withdrew five dollars. A quick peek in the mirror to brush her hair, and she was flying down the stairs and out the side door, barely pausing to lock it behind her.

It was three blocks to the nearest bus stop, but adrenaline carried the girl as if her feet had wings while a plan began to take shape in her mind. It was all so simple—she would journey to the residence of the only person who could possibly understand the predicament of her beloved Beatles and beg for assistance.

* * *

By 1966 Elvis Presley was an American cultural icon, hailed around the world as the King of Rock and Roll by his legions of fans, which not coincidentally included the four boys from Liverpool who called themselves the Beatles.

Born in Tupelo, Mississippi to the humblest of beginnings, Elvis, with his mother and father, had relocated to Memphis when he was thirteen years old. A good-looking, talented singer who had not heeded the criticisms of conservative schoolmates or teachers during his adolescence and carried on with his practice of "rockabilly," an up-tempo blend of country and rhythm and blues, Presley began his career in 1954 at Sun Records in Memphis with producer Sam Phillips, who recognized an opportunity to bring African American music to the greater masses through this talented white entertainer. By 1955 Elvis and his quartet had seen their contract acquired by RCA Victor under agent Colonel Tom Parker, who would oversee Elvis's rise to stardom, beginning with the hit "Heartbreak Hotel" in 1956. A myriad of hit songs, television appearances, and later, movies, would follow. His rockabilly interpretations of popular songs, coupled with a controversially suggestive, gyrating performance style caused girls to swoon, and his appeal to cross racial lines.

Unfortunately, at the height of Elvis's skyrocketing popularity, he was drafted into military service and reported for duty in March of 1958. It was feared by some that Presley's two-year hitch would ruin his career, but the crafty Colonel Parker employed a strategy of sporadically releasing some previously recorded songs over the span that helped Elvis's fans keep him in mind, though he was stationed in Germany for much of his service.

When he returned, Elvis wasn't the white-hot star he was before, but Parker had a solution: Hollywood movies. And so began an incredible string of cinematic vehicles with Elvis as the leading man that would invariably feature Presley songs, some of which climbed to the top of the charts early on. Sometimes there were as many as three films released per year. But by 1966, Elvis had soured on the whole Hollywood scene, hating the modestly budgeted, formulaic light comedies he was featured in, as well as most of the soundtrack music outsiders had created for the films. Ironically, the only songs of his achieving any notoriety during this period were gospel tunes. Of course, as his musical fortunes seemed to be on the decline, the Beatles had climbed to the dizzying heights Elvis had once achieved; rock and roll had changed while The King was making movies.

Marnie and her father, a moderate Elvis fan, had gone to see a few of the films in Memphis, where of course they were met with rousing approval. Marnie's personal favorite was *Viva Las Vegas*, which co-starred the sultry Ann Margaret. Overall, the girl thought Elvis was just fine as a singer, but understandably identified more with her generation's teen idols, the Fab Four.

The week that the Beatles were to visit his hometown, Elvis Presley was entrenched at Graceland, on a break from the filming of *Paradise Hawaiian Style*, yet another movie that would produce lukewarm reviews and no hits, probably wondering if he still had a place in the rapidly evolving music scene he had once dominated. But The King was still a force to be reckoned with, and that was why Marnie Culpeper was hopping aboard the first of three connecting buses that would carry her about nine miles from downtown Memphis to the estate that had become famous around the world. It was the single evocative word *Graceland* that had popped into her mind as she was meditating and she had taken it as a sign, one that she was now impulsively acting upon.

Located on Highway 51 South on nearly 14 acres of rolling farmland, the estate known as Graceland (named after the daughter of the first owner, who had built it in 1939) was a stately two-story Colonial Revival mansion built atop a hill in a grove of oaks. In 1957 Elvis had given his parents Vernon and Gladys a $100,000 budget and asked them to find a property to purchase. At that time, Graceland was located several miles beyond Memphis's main urban area, but by 1966 the city had expanded to the point where it was surrounded by other properties. This necessitated the construction of fences around the sprawling grounds to keep curious fans away from Elvis and his family. Much like the Beatles, Elvis had become a victim of his own success.

Marnie had seen photos of Graceland numerous times and had once passed by with Roy on a Sunday drive. Therefore, she knew that gaining access to the house would be a formidable task. After exiting the bus a block or so away, she went on a reconnaissance mission to see what she was up against.

Upon purchasing the estate, Presley had spent in excess of $500,000 to construct a six-foot pink Alabama fieldstone wall along the front of the property, far removed from the mansion on the hill. The main entrance's wrought iron gate was shaped like a book of sheet music, with green colored musical notes and a silhouette of The King, bookended by large brick pillars. It was a prodigious wall and a deterrent to any kind of frontal assault.

As Marnie walked along, she determined that the fieldstone fence also extended along the sides of the property to the approximate distance of the mansion. Then, a tall white picket fence continued the fortress-like enclosure, with pastureland where horses were grazing stretching a few more acres to the back. She decided that, rather than take a chance of spooking the horses, she would try to climb the stone wall where it broke back from the street towards the house. There, under the cover of some surrounding trees that edged the property, she would be shielded from the eyes of drivers on the road out front and anyone who might be looking out the windows of the house.

Marnie was a good athlete, but even at its lowest point, a little swale around 50 yards from the front left corner, the wall was going to be tough to scale. It was topped with jagged cut pieces of stone which would give her something to grasp but might slice her open if she was indeed able to get on top of the barrier. The last thing she needed was to be found by the Memphis police impaled on Elvis Presley's wall. But there was no turning back. This had to be done, and that was that.

She explored a copse of trees outside the wall and found a section of log that had been left behind when an oak tree had fallen, presumably during a storm. With great effort, she rolled the two-foot long section to within a couple feet of the wall and ground it into the grass. This would serve as a launching platform as she attempted to scale the wall. Now sweating profusely, she backed up some five yards and took some deep breaths. "Okay, here goes nothin'," she said to herself, and took off. Marnie nailed the springboard part perfectly, the log holding fast, but just missed her handhold on the top of the wall and slid down after whacking the fieldstone with her chest.

Marnie sat at the base of the wall, gulping air and checking her scratched elbows. She'd also torn the knees of her Levi's; otherwise, there was no major damage. At this point, most people would have given up; but Marnie Culpeper was not to be denied. She gathered her hair behind her head in a ponytail, retreated to the starting point, inhaled some more deep breaths like a gymnast about to mount a pommel horse, and took off again, this time finding the spiked wall's stones with both hands. After hanging for a couple seconds, she was able to hoist up one leg and hook a Chuck Taylor over the wall, her ankle cracking down on a pointed stone. Then, with more effort and quite a bit of pain, she maneuvered her body over the top and dropped down on the other side, where she lay in a heap, her hands, bare arms and knees scraped and bleeding, until she caught her breath.

The girl rose unsteadily to her feet and made sure she hadn't broken any bones. When everything seemed in order, she began a purposeful walk to the front entrance of the house. What she would find there was anybody's guess.

Over the years, Elvis Presley's fame had led to a gradual withdrawal from the general public in order to preserve some degree of privacy for himself and his family. Graceland became for him a safe, reclusive enclave where he and his handlers/bodyguards, who had been nicknamed "the Memphis Mafia," busied themselves with attending to the needs of their employer while he rode horses, raced golf carts or lounged near his kidney-shaped pool before retreating to his expansive music studio, billiard room or bar. Actually, there wasn't much "work" for any of these men to do except provide security and companionship for Presley and satisfy his every whim.

Whether or not Elvis was even on the premises that day was unknown to Marnie. She was taking a shot in the dark and she knew it. When she approached the majestic front entrance with its projecting portico containing four huge Corinthian columns, she couldn't help but pause in awe. Then, summoning her courage, she mounted four stone steps flanked by two large lion statues, crossed the porch, rang the doorbell and waited.

Nobody answered.

She waited a bit more and pushed the doorbell button again, whispering, "Please, please, please." This time she detected a rustling inside and her heart started thudding in her chest. Was this wild scheme of hers really going to work?

Finally, after a few more agonizing seconds, she heard the sound of a sizable bolt being slid back, and the door opened. A man, most certainly not Elvis, stood in the doorway. He was rather large, though not as muscular as her father, and stern looking. The man was clearly shocked to find this teenaged girl in torn jeans standing on Graceland's front porch. "Young lady, who in the world are you, and what in God's name are you doin' here?" the man asked, taking in her scruffy appearance.

"My name is Marnie Culpeper, sir," she answered, "and I need to talk to Mr. Presley."

"Oh, you do?" asked the man, clearly amused. "And is he expecting you?"

"Uh, not really," she replied, her confidence

beginning to waver. "But I need to speak to him about something very important."

"And what would that be, sugar?"

"It's kind of private."

"Oh, I see," said the man, who was really starting to annoy her. "Well, I'll tell you what. You give me the message and I'll take it to Mr. Presley. That's the only way this is gonna work. You got me?"

"Yeah," she said. "Okay, this is the issue. You know how the Beatles are coming to town tomorrow night at the Coliseum?"

At the mention of their name the bodyguard's eyes widened. "You're here to talk to The King about *them guys*? Are you crazy, girl?"

"No, hear me out, mister," she said, her voice becoming frantic. "You see, the KKK is gonna try to shoot them and I know they look up to Mr. Presley, and, you see, if he could warn them—"

"What'd you say your name was?" interrupted the man.

"Marnie."

"Okay, Marnie, you wait right here. Don't you move, now."

"Okay." He shut the door, and Marnie could hear his footsteps retreating down the front hall. She stood there, sweating in the heat, hoping against hope that Elvis himself would come to the door or even invite her in for a chat, and maybe some lemonade. How cool would *that* be?

But after a few minutes, when the door again opened, it was the same man. "Mister Presley is currently occupied," he said coldly. "I gave him your message. Here, this is for you." He handed her an 8x10 black and white headshot photo of Elvis, inscribed with the words *To Marny, Love, Elvis.* Simultaneously, a golf cart driven by another man pulled up to the front steps. "Lamar will take you out to the gate." With that, he shut the door with a bang.

Marnie stood there trembling with anger for a few humiliating seconds until the man named Lamar called, "Let's go, missie, I don't have all day here." She turned, walked down the steps and climbed into the passenger seat of the golf cart. Both she and the man remained silent during the brief ride to the wrought iron gate. When they got there Lamar took from his pocket a remote device and pushed a button at its center. Magically, the gates began to swing open.

"Young lady," he said, "I don't know how y'all got in here, but do yourself a favor and don't try again, 'cause we'll have to call the po-lice."

"Yes, sir," she said sweetly. "But, could *you* please do me a favor?"

"What's that?"

She tore the 8x10 glossy of The King into little pieces and sprinkled them in his lap. "Just give these to Elvis, would you? I'd really appreciate that."

* * *

Roy entered the packed squad room a step behind Sutter. A semicircle of seated policeman in full uniform, with others shoulder to shoulder standing behind them, quickly heated the room, despite the pedestal fans that were blowing.

"Okay, men," Sutter began, his tone grave. "I need absolute attention from y'all today. We have a detail tomorrow for the concerts at the Mid-South Coliseum that we hope each and every one of you will participate in as gentlemen and officers. Whether you like your detail or whether you do not like your detail…and if you don't like it, let us know about it.

"We hope that you will treat any teenager with all the respect that is possible, but still be demanding in whatever you instruct that person to do and see that it is carried out. I will post the positions of the patrolmen who will be stationed in the aisles, around the stage, at the exits and the upstairs access staircases, as well as outside the dressing room. The musicians will access the stage that has been erected for this event via a rear staircase down the hallway from the dressing room. Now I'll have Sergeant Culpeper address those men who will be guarding the stage."

Roy stepped up, holding the script Sutter had prepared for him. "Men, there is a five-foot chain-link fence that has been put up a few feet in front of the stage. We will position officers every few feet along the inside of the fence. Now, you officers that are stationed behind the barricade, you'll go to the man in charge of first aid, and he will furnish you with earplugs so as to keep you from having a headache. If he runs out of earplugs, he's got some cotton you can use.

"We have a detention room set up within the Coliseum. That detention room is Room D. It is behind the stage. Any person that you arrest or bring downstairs for ejection will be brought to Room D. Is that understood?" There were mumbled responses and nods from the officers. Roy continued, "You will take their names, addresses, and telephone numbers. We will not allow any dancing, running up and down the aisles, or crowding up in front of the stage. All offending parties will be warned and ejected from the Coliseum. Is that clear with all of you? If so, then you are dismissed. Lieutenant Sutter will post the assignments tomorrow morning."

As the meeting broke up, Roy tapped Cecil Blevins on the shoulder and motioned him out into the hallway.

"What's up, Sarge?" asked the amiable patrolman. "Ready to take on an attack of Beatlemania?"

"You'll notice I'm not smiling, Cecil," he answered, which immediately changed the patrolman's demeanor. "I have a bad feeling about tomorrow," he said quietly. "Something just doesn't feel right."

"What do you need from me, Sarge? Just say the word."

"Tomorrow at the Coliseum you'll probably be somewhere on the floor. Keep me in your sight at all times. I might need you at a moment's notice. Can you remember to do that?"

"Sure, Sarge. If I can ask, what in particular are you worried about?"

"Something a little birdie told me. Just be ready if I need you." He patted Cecil on the shoulder and moved off, checking his watch. In eighteen hours the Beatles would land in Memphis.

Chapter Twenty-Seven

Roy Culpeper awakened with a jolt, his bedcovers tangled and his pajamas soaked with sweat. A quick turn towards his alarm clock revealed the time of 2:45 AM. He lay back, trying to slow his heart as it thudded in his chest. He hadn't had this dream in a while, but it had come again, as vivid as ever.

It is winter in Korea, a numbing, gray day, and Roy's platoon has been ordered to take out a North Korean machine gun emplacement that has been raining down bullets on the US troops from atop a craggy hill. Choosing a handful of his best men, Roy claws his way up the hill, bullets pinging off rocks and surrounding trees. By the time he nears the summit, he is the only man left. He tries to circle around to the back of the machine gun nest, where two soldiers are blazing away, one firing the gun while the other feeds a belt of bullets into the breech. Roy manages to get behind the nest, but at the last second, just as he is about to squeeze the trigger of his M-1, the machine gunner detects his presence and turns, simultaneously letting off a burst that catches him squarely in the chest...

Roy tried to fall back asleep but could not, so he lay there awaiting the dawn, the admonition of his commander not to screw things up ringing in his ears.

When the first shafts of light crossed his bedroom window he rose and got dressed, looked in on his daughter, who seemed dead to the world, and eased his way downstairs to make a pot of coffee.

It was going to be a long day.

* * *

While Roy sipped his coffee his daughter, unbeknownst to him, was having dreams of her own, though hardly as violent. Since the Beatles were a constant in her life, it was only natural that they wove their way in and out of her thoughts at night. Most of these dreams were of the teenaged girl fantasy variety, their settings invariably pulled from the Beatles movies she'd seen over and over. A particularly pleasant recurring dream was the one where she and the boys were lounging around the resort pool in the Bahamas from *Help!* where they had dramatically surfaced while escaping from the clutches of the evil Eastern high priest named Klang. Or maybe she was skiing down the slopes of the Austrian Alps with them, laughing all the way. Usually, though, she would end up in the recording studio with the group, watching with rapt attention as they performed a song—usually a romantic one like "And I Love Her" for her benefit. Sometimes she even sang along.

But tonight's dream was different.

She was alone, walking along a dimly lit hallway. It was still and somewhat cool, despite the fact that she was in jeans and some kind of long-sleeved top. She moved forward, past closed industrial-looking doors, trying the metal pull-type handles one after another, with no success. But then she heard faint conversation and laughter from one of the rooms, and opened the heavy door, which swung open on its hinges.

The Beatles were sitting in chairs around a small coffee-style table, wearing the matching black turtlenecks of their *Meet the Beatles* album cover, dark pants and Beatle boots. John, Paul and George were holding acoustic guitars on their laps, and Ringo had a pair of drumsticks he was fiddling with. Scraps of paper with what appeared to be song lyrics littered the coffee table, along with half-finished cups of tea. John was half-murmuring a song to the others as he, Paul and George seemed to be working out the chords. It all seemed very casual and relaxed, and they appeared to be enjoying themselves.

Lennon was the first one to acknowledge her presence. "Well, if it isn't the famous heretic, Marnie Culpeper," he cracked. "So nice to see you."

"Hey, c'mon," said Paul to his friend, "it's you that got her in this mess, so that'll be enough of that."

"Yeah, Marnie," said George, "come join us. We've saved a seat for you."

"So, uh, what are you doing?" she asked, easing into a chair.

"Working out some new material," John replied. "I think you'll like it…or maybe not. It's all a matter of taste, y'know. But it'll be different, that's for certain."

"Like *Revolver*?"

"Yeah, but better. You'll see."

Paul fixed upon her with his doe eyes. "Truthfully, Marnie, do you like what we've been up to?"

"Well, uh, it's just not what I'm used to," she said. "I've got to listen a few times to understand it."

"That's the whole idea," John said with a sniff. "I mean, you're getting too grown up for the 'yeah, yeah, yeah' bit, aren't you?"

"I suppose," she admitted, "but I still kinda like your older stuff."

"That's fine, y'know," Ringo said with a smile. "And personally, I'm just happy you're buying our records!"

"Yeah," Paul said with his most winning smile. "Thanks for supporting us."

"You're welcome," she said, finally relaxing a bit, although she had her doubts about what she'd just been hearing. A song about *strawberries*? *Really*?

Then John strummed a few more chords and said, "So what's this about you not coming to the concert?"

"It's true," she replied. "I've been grounded for shooting my mouth off in church."

"So, we won't be seeing you, then?"

"I don't know. Maybe next time."

"What if there is no next time?"

Marnie panicked. Did John know about the KKK threat? How could he, possibly? Should she warn him? "Why wouldn't there be a next time?" she asked nervously.

"There could be a lot of reasons," George said ambiguously.

"Yeah, tomorrow never knows," Ringo said, smiling at his reference.

"What we're saying is, we really need you there," Paul said.

"Yeah, try and make it, okay?" John added. "It would be a drag if you didn't."

"I'll try," she promised.

"Then we'll be off," John said, grinning at her for the first time. "Goodbye, Marnie Culpeper." In a blink all four of them dissolved before she could get another word out, leaving her alone in the somewhat cramped room. She momentarily considered scooping up the lyric notes as souvenirs, but then thought better of it and turned to leave. But when she tried the door it wouldn't budge. She was locked in. She started pounding on the metal door, calling for help, when she was suddenly awakened by the sound of Tillie yelling up to her from the kitchen. "Marnie!" she called. "I've been keepin' your breakfast warm over an hour. You gonna eat it or not?"

She glanced over at her alarm clock. It was 9 AM. *Wow, that was so real. I still have a chill from that room.*

She sat up and called down to Tillie, "I'll be right there! Sorry!" and shuffled off to the bathroom, forgetting to start the record player for the first time in months.

There were eleven hours left until the concert.

* * *

The Beatles' flight from Boston to Memphis was a somber one, fraught with tension. Earlier that morning Brian Epstein had received a phone call from someone threatening to kill one or more members of the group. The Beatles sat together on the packed American Airlines charter flight, staring out the windows as they approached the home of their hero, Elvis Presley.

"So, this is where all the Christians come from," John Lennon said mirthlessly.

Paul McCartney, sitting next to him, succinctly replied, "You're a very controversial person."

Only George Harrison could add some of the famous Beatle levity to the ominous situation. "Send John out first," he cracked, "he's the one they want."

"You might as well paint a target on me," Lennon concluded glumly.

The plane touched down on the steaming tarmac, a great distance from the terminal or any fans that might have shown up. Policemen were everywhere. An officer who introduced himself as Lieutenant Joe Bob Sutter was there to officially greet the entourage, wearing aviator sunglasses and a smile that accentuated the wine stain along his jaw. "Welcome to Memphis, boys," he drawled. "Hope it isn't too hot for y'all."

The Beatles, all of whom were wearing sport jackets and long pants, smiled tightly.

"Okay, then, we've got this fine Wells Fargo truck for the four of you, and a city bus for the rest of your group." Lieutenant Sutter pointed to a large vehicle with enough room for Epstein, Tony Barrow, Neil Aspinall, Mal Evans, the other acts' performers and all the equipment. The party made their way to the bus, muttering about the quality of their transportation. Once they were aboard, Sutter climbed the stairs to the seating area and announced, "We'd appreciate it if y'all keep the windows closed and stay down in your seats. Wouldn't want some nutcase takin' a potshot at you," he said, pointing his finger like a pistol.

Then, the smiling lieutenant approached the Beatles, who stood baking on the tarmac. He opened the rear panel doors to the armored truck and gaily announced, "Here we go, fellas. Just sit on the floor and make y'selves as comfortable as possible. This is all for your own protection. And don't fret about the heat in the truck. We'll be at the Coliseum in no time." The Fab Four looked at each other, shrugged, and climbed in as they were told. This wasn't the movie *Help!* where bumbling crackpots were trying to do them in; this was actually a matter of life and death.

The convoy, surrounded by motorcycles and bookended by police cruisers, then wound its way to the Coliseum, passing roadside protesters and fans alike on the way. Some of the anti-Beatles people held signs that said **Beatles Go Home** and **Jesus Died for YOUR Sins, John Lennon!**

When they pulled into the Coliseum's parking lot, headed for the service entrance at the rear, Epstein and the other bus people could see, even at this early hour, an odd assortment of people milling around. There were teenagers with crew cuts toting anti-Beatles slogans, others in bell- bottomed jeans with longer hair holding Beatles paraphernalia for autographing and, incredibly, a handful of Ku Klux Klan members in full costume.

Roy Culpeper, who was traversing the parking lot with some patrolmen to make sure nothing got out of hand, happened upon a Klansman who was being interviewed by a tape recorder-toting reporter, who held a small microphone to the man's mouth.

The Klansman, with his face flap raised but wearing sunglasses, declared, "The Beatles made a statement in all the newspapers that they're getting more better than Jesus himself. And the Ku Klux Klan, being a religious order, is gonna come out here the night that they appear in the Coliseum here and we're gonna demonstrate with, uh, different ways and tactics to stop this performance. The Klan is going to come out here because we're the only organization that will come out and make a stop to these accusations. This is nothing but blasphemy, and we're gonna try to stop it any way we can. We are known as a terror organization—"

"A terror organization?" broke in the reporter.

The Klansman flashed a chilling smile. "We have ways and means to stop this if this is gonna be the case."

The reporter asked, "By what 'ways and means'?"

"Well, I don't want to say this, but, uh, there'll be a lot of surprises."

Roy moved on, deeply concerned, and entered the Coliseum to begin preparing for the first concert, which was to kick off at 4 PM with the opening acts.

* * *

With an eye peeled to watch Tillie, who was in the backyard hanging wash on the clothes line, Marnie hurriedly dialed the number Myles had given her earlier in the week. When the receptionist at Mr. Goldfarb's office answered, she asked for his son.

"Please hold for a minute while I find him," she said pertly.

"Thank you," said Marnie, thinking *Come on, come on, I don't have all day here.*

"Hello, this is Myles Goldfarb, may I help you?" the boy said, sounding very official.

"Myles, it's me," Marnie said. "Listen, I've gotta

be quick so Tillie doesn't catch me on the phone. You're still picking me up tonight, right?"

"Well, my dad is, yeah. He'll be dropping us off at the Coliseum. What time?"

"We've got to cut it close and slip in…the concert starts at 8:30, so how about 8 PM?"

"That's cool. Hey, are you still sure you want to do this?"

"Myles, I *have* to. I had this dream last night, and I don't have time to tell you all the details now, but at the end I was talking to John Lennon and he said, "Goodbye, Marnie Culpeper.""

"You mean, you had like a premonition thing?"

"Yeah. It was really creepy. Oh-oh, here comes Tillie. Gotta go. See you at eight."

"Gotcha."

She hung up and busied herself with looking in the fridge as Tillie came in, carrying the empty laundry hamper. "Lordy, it's hot as blazes out there today," she said, wiping her brow. "Good thing you're stayin' inside."

The evening concert was eight hours away.

* * *

As the road crew set up the Beatles' amplifiers and Ringo's drum kit on the stage (due to the lack of a sophisticated sound system, the Beatles would have to run their woefully weak Vox amplifiers through the Coliseum's PA system), Lt. Sutter handed Roy the detail list for the Coliseum interior during the concerts. He was happy to see that Cecil, assigned a position at the rear of one of the floor aisles, would be within hailing distance. What bothered him, though, was that patrolmen Mathews and Stevens, the two jokers from the Perkins Market incident who had reported his intervention to Sutter, were stationed at the access stairways to the upper level. Why had *they* been chosen? Was it just a coincidence?

Roy, via his walkie-talkie, would be in contact not only with Sutter, but the first aid station, which would be manned with paramedic personnel to attend to any injured or fainting teens, and the patrolman in charge of the backstage area and dressing rooms. He decided to try to sneak another walkie-talkie to Cecil, just in case. Then he wandered around, checking in with his officers, making sure that the ones positioned stage-side had their earplugs, and then ventured backstage to visit with the patrolman there. "Where are they?" he asked the officer, whose name was Lyons.

"In the dressing room, Sarge," Lyons replied. "Trying to relax, I guess."

Roy nodded and let himself in. Lennon and McCartney were seated on folding chairs facing each other, holding acoustic guitars and strumming some chords as they conversed. Harrison was stretched out on a lounge chair, and Starr was in conversation with Brian Epstein. All were in casual shirts and jeans, the dark suits with open-necked dress shirts they would wear for the afternoon concert neatly pressed and hanging on a rolling coat rack. He approached Epstein, whom he recognized from television clips. "Is there anything the boys need?" he asked in a tone far different from the condescending one used by Sutter earlier.

The Beatles' manager, in his polished, upper-crust British accent, answered, "It seems we're set,

Sergeant. The sandwiches were fine and we have enough cold soft drinks to last us. How is it going out there?"

At these words the Beatles, especially Lennon, seemed to perk up their ears, and Roy noticed. "We're putting our men in place. Overall, there will be around 80 personnel deployed in the arena."

"That's fine, Sergeant," Epstein said, "but the boys would rather not see some of the aggressive behavior displayed in some of the earlier concerts of the tour. These fans are here to enjoy themselves, after all."

"I understand. We'll do our best," he assured the manager.

"And, to be clear, this will be a totally integrated audience, as per the stipulation of our contract with the promoter?"

"This concert was open to anyone who wanted to purchase a ticket, that's what I was told," Roy stated. "How many colored folks show up is anyone's guess. But I assure you, those who do will be given the same consideration as the white patrons."

"That's all we can ask for," Epstein said, extending his hand, which Roy shook. "Thank you very much, Sergeant."

"I'll look in on you between shows," Roy said. "If you need anything until then, tell patrolman Lyons, and he will contact me via walkie-talkie."

"Righto, and thanks again."

Roy made eye contact with Lennon, who was wearing dark horn-rimmed glasses, and nodded. Lennon nodded back. McCartney gave him a smile and a thumbs-up.

Upon exiting the dressing room, Roy resumed his rounds, checking his watch constantly, and encountered Cecil Blevins, who was sipping some coffee from a paper cup. "Guess what, Cecil," he said, "I just met the Beatles."

"No kidding, Sarge? What were they like?"

"Just seemed like normal guys with a lot of hair. Boy howdy, if Marnie had been there, she'd have been going crazy. Either that or she'd pass out from shock." He paused and looked down.

"You having second thoughts about keeping her home tonight?"

"I don't know. I'll tell you, this parenting thing isn't easy. Sometimes it feels wrong no matter what you do. You'll find that out when you have kids yourself."

"Gotta get someone to marry me first," the patrolman joked. Then his tone turned serious. "You happy with the setup here?"

"Pretty much, except I don't like Stevens and Mathews at the upstairs access staircases."

"They're a couple of wrong numbers, that's for sure," Cecil said. "What, you think they're gonna slack off or somethin'?"

"Can't be sure. That's why I'm giving you this." He handed Blevins a walkie-talkie. "If you see anything hinky goin' on, you let me know." He checked his watch. "It's 3:30. Crowd should be comin' in any minute."

"You need me, Sarge, I'll be there," Cecil assured him.

* * *

At 3:30 PM the doors opened and joyous Beatle fans flooded in. Though there seemed to be some pockets of empty seats, the arena, which consisted of the huge floor section and two mezzanines flanking the floor, appeared mostly full.

"Are we ready, Sergeant?" Sutter asked. He seemed on edge.

"Yes, sir. Everyone's in place."

"Stay on top of it."

"Yes, sir."

With a pair of binoculars Roy kept checking the aisles of both the floor and the mezzanine, counting the officers over and over, looking for any rowdy behavior. The opening acts, consisting this day of the Remains, the Cyrcle, and Bobby Hebb, did their best to occupy the crowd, who at times got a "We want the Beatles!" chant going, drowning out their performances. Roy was astounded at the devotion of the Beatle fans, especially the girls, and began to understand his own daughter's passion. Again, he felt a pang of regret for grounding her.

When the Beatles finally took the stage, it was pandemonium. Roy had never experienced noise like this in his life, not even when under artillery fire in Korea. Perhaps it was because the sound was bouncing off the domed roof and coming back down. With every movement, every shake of the head, every smile or wave from the boys, the decibel level rose another notch. It hardly mattered which song they were playing (to Roy they mostly seemed the same anyway). As soon as the opening chord for each song was struck, it felt like the Coliseum's roof was going to blow off. The only respite from the noise was when Paul McCartney sang

"Yesterday," a song he'd heard on the radio. Roy personally checked on Stevens and Mathews twice during the performance to find them sitting, somewhat bored, on the steps of their respective staircases.

And then, suddenly, with a final explosion of sound, the Beatles' set was done. It had taken but a half hour. The delirious crowd was herded towards the exits and Roy went to check on the detention room and first aid station. Aside from a couple of kids detained for jumping on their chairs and a few fainters (all girls, of course) it had gone remarkably smoothly.

He was halfway home.

* * *

The Beatles were understandably relaxed and upbeat between the shows. Despite some empty seats, those fans who had shown up were loud and overwhelmingly supportive, with girls crying and screaming and throwing gifts such as stuffed animals on the stage. Now they unwound, enjoying a roast beef dinner before entertaining some reporters. Mal Evans even drew some laughs when he produced a local newspaper with an ad that read, "Go to church on Sunday, but see the Beatles Friday!"

The group then sat for an interview with Richard Lindley of the ITV program *Reporting 66* as part of a documentary to be called *The Beatles Across America.* They were, of course, asked if the recent Jesus controversy had contributed to a loss in ticket sales, but they shrugged it off, as well as the antics of the Birmingham deejays Charles and Layton, which they deemed as childish.

When asked if they felt Americans were "out to get them," and if things were taking on the feel of a "witch hunt," Paul McCartney replied, "No. We thought it might be that kind of thing…you know, when America gets violent and gets very hung up on a thing, it tends to have this sort of 'Ku Klux Klan' thing around it." And then, again, the Beatles registered their disapproval of the Vietnam War.

Lennon concluded the interview by saying, "It doesn't matter about people not liking our records, or not liking the way we look, or what we say. You know, they're entitled not to like us. And we're entitled not to have anything to do with them if we don't want to, or not to regard them. We've all got our rights, you know…"

* * *

At precisely 8:00 PM Mr. Goldfarb, with Myles in the passenger seat, eased the huge Cadillac Eldorado to the curb in front of the Culpeper residence and gave a little honk. Marnie bounded out the front door and climbed into the spacious, air-conditioned luxury car.

"Hi there, Marnie," Myles's father said. "Are you excited? I know you're quite the Beatles fan."

"Oh yes, definitely," she replied. "I've been looking forward to tonight for a long time. It was so nice of Myles to give me the ticket."

"My pleasure," said the boy gallantly from the plush front seat.

They tooled along, the radio tuned to WHBQ which, in honor of the concerts, was playing Beatles records. Marnie was pleased her hometown station had not buckled to pressure and boycotted the Beatles like many other stations across the South. She even had hopes that the evening would go smoothly. But these hopes were dashed when Mr. Goldfarb turned into the vast parking lot outside the Coliseum and was immediately confronted by a group of Ku Klux Klansmen in full dress, carrying signs protesting the Beatles and handing out leaflets to last-minute arrivals like themselves, urging them to burn their Beatles paraphernalia. Mr. Goldfarb, gritting his teeth, calmly navigated the boat-like vehicle past the Klansmen and dropped the teens off outside the main entrance. "You be careful now," he cautioned. "Keep an eye out for these nuts and tell the police if anyone harasses you."

"We will, Dad," Myles promised.

"I'll be here by eleven to pick you up," Mr. Goldfarb said. "If I have to wait a bit, so be it."

Marnie and Myles exited the car and shut the heavy doors. As the Eldorado pulled away from the curb Myles turned to Marnie. "Okay, so now what do we do?"

* * *

Meanwhile, across town, the Christian rally was coming together. In a *Commercial Appeal* interview, the Rev. James E. Hamill, pastor of the First Assembly of God Church, had said that "Memphis is the only city in America doing something positive in a rally while the Beatles are in the towns…they have challenged the church of Jesus Christ. We are not going to lie down and roll over. It is time to stand up and be counted, and we believe the youth of Memphis and the Mid-South are ready to meet this challenge by making this rally the biggest ever in the city."

Then, in an interview to the *Commercial Appeal's* chief rival, the *Press-Scimitar*, Hamill declared that the Beatles "have insulted the Christian community. They owe more than the apology that was made. This rally will present an opportunity for true Christians to make a statement."

By the time the rally got started, the crowd numbered upwards of 8,000—half of them adults. Those teens whom were in attendance were dressed modestly and well-groomed, but they applauded passionately during the many speeches and testimonials. The featured pastor, Reverend Jimmy Stroud, received a spirited response when he said, "Concerning the purpose of this rally, I thank God that Jesus Christ is popular with me because he saved me 31 years ago; and everyone who's here, if he's popular with you, say amen!" Everywhere in the crowd, people were standing and thrusting their hands skyward. Two of the non-clergy guest speakers were even given the keys to the city by Memphis Mayor William B. Ingram, who had refused to bestow that same honor upon the Beatles.

Oddly, though, some of the adults who were present actually walked out on a performance by a group called Sing-Out Memphis when they did a couple of religious songs with an up-tempo beat, obviously trying to appeal to the youngsters in the audience. One parent complained that they had been "decoyed" into going to what was supposed to be a Christian service, only to see Sing-Out Memphis belting out a pop-style song while performing a dance move vaguely resembling the Twist.

Reverend Hollis, who was seated with the other prominent clergymen, was extremely pleased with the turnout, though he considered the choice of music unfortunate.

At the same time, at the back of the auditorium, Lt. Joe Bob Sutter, overseeing the handful of officers deployed in the auditorium for "crowd control," smiled at the behavior of the huge gathering, and checked his watch.

* * *

"Marnie? Hello? I asked you what we're going to do."

"I know, Myles, I'm just thinking. Tell you what, let's go in and check out where the police are. My guess is that my father is near the stage, but a lot of these guys know who I am, and so…" She pulled from her back pocket her tattered Tennessee Vols hat and pulled it down low on her brow. To finish the disguise, she added a pair of sunglasses.

"Wow, you're like the Girl from U.N.C.L.E.," complimented Myles.

"I wish. Let's get after it."

By this time most of the crowd were in their seats, waiting anxiously for the first act, noisily buzzing in anticipation, so Marnie and Myles passed through the turnstiles quickly, the ticket takers ripping the cardboard in half and handing them back the stubs. Then she turned to him. "Okay, Myles, so here it is: do you agree we're here for a more important reason than seeing the concert?"

"Well, yeah," he said.

"Great. Then you need to go to the bathroom."

"*What?*"

"Listen, it's only 8:30. There's a few acts that have to go on before the Beatles. So, we're gonna hide out in the bathrooms until we hear the crowd going crazy. That'll mean the Beatles are coming on."

"The bathroom," he repeated.

"Yeah, the bathroom. The longer I hang out in the open, the better chance there is of someone seeing me. We have to time it just right."

"Time what?"

"We have to get up to the upper level, above the stands where it's facing the stage. If someone's gonna take a shot at them, I bet that's where they'll be. Up high and undetected."

"Are you sure?"

"That's what Oswald did with JFK, right?"

"I guess so. But what if we *do* see someone with a rifle?"

"*Then* we run for the police and I don't care if my daddy finds out."

"You think it'll work?"

"You have a better idea?"

"Nope."

"Then it's off to the bathrooms. Fortunately, they're close together, just a little ways to the left. Pick a stall and have a seat."

"I wish you'd told me about this earlier," he grumbled. "I would've at least brought a magazine to read."

* * *

For the second time today, Roy and his officers had to endure the tedium of the three opening acts before the main event. Predictably, by the last singer, Bobby Hebb, the crowd had grown restless and started the "We Want the Beatles!" chant. He actually felt sorry for the other performers. He was equally mystified and impressed at the power the Beatles wielded over their audience, the absolute devotion and hysteria that had the first girls dropping in a dead faint before they had even taken the stage. Roy had listened carefully to Hebb's set the first time to know when he was nearly done. It was time to get on the walkie-talkie. "Cecil," he said, "do you read me, over?"

"Yeah, Sarge, I'm here," drawled the officer. "What do you need?"

"Go to the staircase on the ground floor near section G-N. See if there's an officer stationed there. I'll be on the opposite side, the stairs near section H-S. Call me after you check it out, over."

"Roger, Sarge."

Roy quickly strode out of the seating area to the semicircular corridor of the main entrance side and hustled to the staircase at section H-S.

It was unmanned.

Seconds later, his walkie-talkie crackled with the sound of Blevins's voice. "Nobody here, Sarge," he reported. "Wasn't Mathews and Stevens supposed to be on the staircases?"

Not if someone pulled them off it, thought Roy. "Okay, Cecil," he said, "now listen sharp. There's a lot of rooms up top of this place, storage rooms and whatever. I went up there this morning before anyone got here and had a janitor open them up for me, just in case. I'm afraid we got a shooter up there somewhere—"

Suddenly a sound emanated from the arena like a

jet plane taking off, rendering Cecil's walkie-talkie useless. The Beatles were taking the stage. "Sarge!" he screamed into the mouthpiece, "hold on! I've gotta go somewhere I can hear!" He bolted towards the men's room and almost ran over a gangly boy who was hurriedly walking out. "Okay, what did you say?" he barked, a finger plugging his other ear.

"I said, I think we got a shooter upstairs! Get your butt up there and look for a closed door. Work your way towards me, 'cause I'll be comin' the other way. Do you read me, over?"

"Roger! I'm on my way!"

He hadn't seen the gangly boy and the girl as they pounded up the staircase a minute ahead of him.

* * *

The upstairs corridor was disorienting to Marnie and Myles, threateningly dark and narrow. And the deafening clamor as the Beatles were being introduced by a local deejay was making the building shake around them. They could barely make out the open doorways of rooms that served as storage closets or offices for various Coliseum custodial or concessions personnel during the daytime hours. As they feverishly began searching the small rooms, Marnie's trained ear could pick out the opening strains of "Rock and Roll Music" that caused the crowd noise to rise even a few more levels. They were just ducking into the third entrance when a shadow came from behind a huge metal cabinet and flung them into the wall of the cramped room. Myles hit the plaster surface with a sickening crack. Marnie toppled over him and struck the wall with the side of her head, temporarily stunning her and allowing their attacker to exit the room, slamming the door behind him.

In the pitch black, Marnie shook off the cobwebs, not knowing if she'd been out for seconds or minutes. She felt Myles underneath her and jostled him while calling his name. She was horrified to feel what had to be blood. "Oh, Myles, what did I get you into?" she said with a moan. Then she was on her feet, the pain in her head ringing as she began feeling for the door. When it wouldn't budge she started pounding on it, screaming for help. But the Beatles and their wildly enthusiastic fans had created such a wall of sound that the thought of anyone coming to save them seemed hopeless.

* * *

When Roy got to the top of the stairwell, he cursed aloud. Whereas the lights had been turned on this morning for him, the curving corridor was now dark and shadowy. He could, however, barely discern whether the doors to the closets were open. Which they were, until he reached section C-S, nearly dead-on to the front of the stage.

It was locked tight.

Quickly deciding there was no time to waste, Roy drew his service revolver and blasted the door handle, with a sound that reverberated in the hallway but was lost in the overall din of the arena. However, the lighting was so poor that it took multiple rounds for him to hit it right. Then he backed up, lowered his shoulder and rammed the door, practically knocking it off its hinges.

The sniper's nest lay before him, a hooded shooter seated on a box with his rifle resting on some others, its barrel protruding through a hole that had been cut in the thin drywall. Barely recovered from the impact of hitting the door, Roy charged ahead as the surprised executioner turned, leveling the rifle at the policeman's chest.

* * *

With the darkness and all the noise assaulting his eardrums, Cecil Blevins nearly bypassed the closed door—until the sound of frantic pounding drew him to it. The door was not locked but had a piece of scrap wood jammed beneath it. He took a breath, pulled his revolver (which he'd never had cause to do to this point in the line of duty), kicked the wedge out of the way and threw the door open, holding the pistol in front of him while assuming the shooter's crouch he'd learned in basic training. Thus, he was shocked when a screaming girl tumbled out and hit the floor, her Tennessee Vols cap flying off.

"Punkin'," he said breathlessly, "what in tarnation are *you* doin' here?"

* * *

On stage, things were going well for the Beatles who, buoyed by the success of the first concert, had kicked off the set with a spirited rendition of "Rock and Roll Music," after which Paul McCartney, acting as MC, had enthusiastically introduced their second number, "She's a Woman," which again ratcheted up the screaming. All four of them, resplendent in light green pinstriped suits with open-necked shirts for the second show, were smiling and having a good time, the finish line in sight.

They were barely underway in the next song, George Harrison's "If I Needed Someone," when a shot rang out.

* * *

Roy Culpeper's recurring nightmare seemed to be coming alive, though a hooded rifleman had replaced the North Korean machine gunners and the Coliseum's upper level the hilltop. But unlike in Roy's dream, he was quicker than his adversary, catching him underneath the gun barrel in the solar plexus and driving him back into the boxes that were serving as the sniper's nest, the rifle discharging upwards into the low ceiling. Roy grabbed the still-smoking barrel of the weapon, and was trying to wrest it from the shooter, when someone stepped up from behind and knocked him senseless.

* * *

Cecil was busy picking Marnie off the floor when they heard a *pop-pop-pop-boom-BOOM!*

"They're shooting the Beatles!" she moaned.

"Or someone else," said Cecil, taking off down the hallway with his gun drawn.

* * *

When the explosion occurred, Paul McCartney, George Harrison and Ringo Starr momentarily froze and looked towards John Lennon, whom they assumed had been shot, but Lennon was still at the microphone, in his familiar legs-apart stance, guitar in hand. He gave his mates a quick look and kept playing, smoke drifting upwards from the cherry bomb a prankster in the audience had thrown on the stage, where it had gone off near the riser of Ringo's drum kit. They finished George's number, hardly skipping a beat, and pressed on with the set.

* * *

Cecil, with a wobbly Marnie in tow, kept running until the heavy smell of cordite assaulted his nostrils. Then he spied a door that was crookedly hanging and kicked it wider open, only to find Roy faced down on the floor, his service revolver at his side.

"Daddy!" Marnie screamed, throwing herself upon the stricken policeman. Cecil immediately got on the walkie-talkie and announced a man down on the top floor. Fearing the worst, he peeled the sobbing girl off her father and turned him over.

"Sarge?" he called, gently shaking his shoulder. "Sarge, you okay?"

After a few agonizing seconds, Roy's eyelids began fluttering, and then opened. "Little girl, what are *you* doing here?" he croaked.

"Oh, Daddy, Daddy," she cried, again falling on top of him, "you're alive? Oh, thank you, God, thank you, God!"

"Can you sit up, Sarge?" asked Blevins.

"Let me try," he replied. "Marnie, help me." Slowly, she eased his shoulders off the ground. "Owww, my head," he said with a loud moan. "The room's spinnin'."

"What happened?" Cecil asked.

"There…was a shooter," he said haltingly, trying to blink away the dizziness, "just like I thought. Couldn't see who. I got to him just in time, I think…then someone whacked me from behind and I heard, 'Let's get outta here!' before I blacked out. I *did* get there in time, didn't I?"

Marnie and Cecil exchanged a look. "I don't know, Daddy," she snuffled. "I heard a pretty loud *boom* that came from inside the arena."

Suddenly, a paramedic, flanked by Memphis PD patrolmen, was sprinting towards them, followed by two more attendants with a rolling stretcher.

"Oh, my God!" blurted Marnie, totally frazzled, "I forgot about Myles! Come with me, please!" She took off back down the hallway, followed by the paramedics.

Roy, now a little more lucid, climbed to his feet, holding onto Blevins for support, and turned to one of the officers. "Were there shots fired in the auditorium?" he asked.

"Nah, Sarge," he replied with a smile. "Dangdest thing, though. Two kids lit a cherry bomb and chucked it on stage while the Beatles were singin'. I have to give it to those boys, they hardly missed a note! Don't worry, we nabbed the kids."

"Good job," Roy said wearily.

"Here comes your daughter," Cecil said. "Who's that with her on the gurney?"

"Oh, no," Roy said, fearing the worst. But Myles Goldfarb was far from dead. He lay awake on his back, an apparently fractured wrist immobilized and some dried blood on his face where he'd bitten through his lip when he hit the wall. But he was smiling, and that was promising.

"Hi, Mr. Culpeper," he said sheepishly.

Marnie looked around at all the assembled personnel and whispered, "Did the Beatles get shot?"

"No, baby girl, they're fine," her father said, holding an ice pack to the back of his head.

"You saved them, Daddy," she said, hugging him tightly.

"We all did. Now let's get out of here and take care of Myles."

* * *

Some minutes later, they were all downstairs in the recesses of the lower level, except for Myles, who was being tended to in the first aid station. It was blessedly quiet, with most of the crowd having filed out. Roy was checking in with his officers. As he suspected, someone had radioed Stevens and Mathews to pull them off their posts. At least, that was what they told him. When Roy asked who it was, they said they couldn't tell due to the extreme noise in the building. He then called Cecil aside and told him not to breathe a word to anyone of what had happened with him or the teens.

"But why, Sarge?" Blevins asked incredulously. "You're a hero!"

"Just trust me on this one, Cecil," he said, noting

that his superior officer had yet to return to the Coliseum. "But I have to tell you, partner, you did real good."

Blevins smiled proudly.

"Daddy," Marnie said, interrupting him, "Myles's dad is probably outside in the parking lot waiting for us. Should I go get him?"

"Might as well," he replied. "I need to have a word with him, and I suppose he'll have to run Myles over to the hospital for some x-rays." As she briskly walked away, Roy, his energy sapped, leaned back against the cinderblock wall and closed his eyes.

"That's some girl you got there, Sarge," said Cecil admiringly.

"I know," he replied. "I'm just so danged tired."

The patrolman smiled. "Hey, Sarge, what's it those Beatles say? It's been a hard day's night."

* * *

Since they were adjacent to the bowels of the building, Marnie decided to exit via one of the service ramps. When she approached the garage door-like opening, a huge black Cadillac was sitting just inside, its engine idling. As Marnie got closer, she deduced that it must be the Beatles' limousine to the airport. She had just reached the rear passenger side window when it started to pull away, but not before John Lennon, looking both relieved and exhausted, offered a fleeting wave.

Epilogue
August 19, 2016

"Ladies first," Myles said, holding the door open.

Marnie stepped inside and a chill ran up her spine. So many ghosts. So many memories. "Let's walk around," she suggested.

"Lead the way," he said. "I'll follow you, just like the old days."

Even though the electricity had long since been shut off in the facility, there was some ambient light, shafts of brightness here and there from the dirty windows as they strolled around the lower concourse hallway. It was lined with concession stands, their front pull-down corrugated screens shut tight, but some of the signs were still in place, advertising prices for food items from 2006. Rodent tracks crisscrossed the dusty floors.

"Remember hiding out in the bathrooms?" Marnie asked, pointing at the adjacent restroom entrances to the left of the main entrance.

"Yeah. I had a lot of time to get good and nervous, as I recall."

"Me too."

They entered the arena at the floor level, across from where the stage had been erected. The bench seating from 1966 had been replaced with blue and red plastic riser mount chairs, forming a multi-colored bowl. A 1980s vintage Jumbotron scoreboard hung from the center of the white domed ceiling, which was now missing quite a few of its interior panels. A large American flag hung down as well.

"Remember the noise that night?" Marnie said, reminiscing. "How god-awful loud it was? I could hardly hear myself think."

"That's because it was just about a full house," Myles recalled, "and it seemed like every single person inside here was screaming their heads off. Of course, then I got knocked out, but even so, I remember the vibrations before the paramedics brought me fully around."

"Does the wrist ever bother you?"

"Not really. And I still play tennis, as badly as ever," he joked.

"It seemed like every teenager in Memphis was here," she said. "Hard to believe that Christian rally across town supposedly had like 8,000 people at it."

"Did anyone you know go to it?"

"Yeah, Charlotte Perkins. Remember her?"

"Sure I do. But she didn't graduate with us from Central, did she?"

"Nope. After tenth grade her daddy pulled her out and sent her to a private school. We'd kind of drifted apart by then anyway, but I sometimes regret that we fell out of touch after that. I have no idea what happened to her."

"You can always do the Google thing and find her."

"Yeah, I guess. The question is, what would I say to her when I did? Maybe someday."

They crossed the empty space on the arena floor where the folding chairs had been set up for the Beatles concert. It was covered with dust, fallen ceiling panels, and various other debris. "What about that other girl?" Myles said suddenly. "You know, the mean one, whatshername."

"Betty Lou?"

"Yeah, the one who made your life miserable."

"Ah, yes. Well, you remember that in high school she eventually became captain of the cheerleading squad—"

"Her lifelong dream, I would imagine."

"Uh-huh. And she didn't waste any time stealing Tommy Plummer away from Charlotte once he became the varsity quarterback. But I guess karma came back to bite her on the butt, because if you remember, she suddenly disappeared in the spring of our senior year. From what I found out, Tommy got her pregnant, and they had to get married—that's what you did in those days—so his football scholarship went out the window. Rumor has it she and Tommy have like five kids now and live in a trailer park outside the city, and she has to work at Walmart to support the family."

"Wow," he said. "No wonder neither of them have been to any of our class reunions."

"Yeah, well, I haven't, either," she said. "I just haven't seen the point." Her words hung in the air.

"Want to go upstairs?" he asked.

"Might as well."

They exited to the concourse and made their way to the staircase they'd dashed up in 1966. The upper level was predictably dark, but Myles had come prepared and produced a small flashlight. They started walking, hand-in-hand. "Here's the room we got locked in," he said, shining the flashlight inside the barren space. "Just looking in here gives me the creeps."

"Let's keep going," she suggested.

Finally, they came upon the room where Roy Culpeper had encountered the assassin. Though the door was open, it was easy to tell that it was a replacement for the one he had splintered that night with his gun and shoulder. The room was now devoid of any boxes or other signs of habitation, an empty shell—though the chilling opening that had been created for the rifle barrel remained.

They stood there for a few seconds in the near darkness. Myles said, "I wonder what happened to our friend Lt. Sutter?"

"Well," she replied, "both Daddy and I knew he had something to do with arranging the shooting attempt, although he made sure he was across town when it happened. But Daddy also knew he couldn't pin anything on Sutter, and that if he tried, he'd probably end up ruining his own career."

"So, he got away with it."

"Yes and no," she said. "It took a couple more years, but then Sutter screwed up, just like Daddy figured he would. You see, although we were pretty sure he wasn't personally involved, Sutter messed up his assignment during the Martin Luther King assassination in '68 at the Lorraine Motel so badly that he was dismissed from the force—something about contaminating the crime scene that got the FBI in an uproar about his ineptitude. Funny thing, though. In

1993 a white man from Memphis named Lloyd Jowers gained some attention for claiming the shooter was, among other people, a 'white lieutenant' in the Memphis Police Department. So anyway, Sutter got thrown off the force and supposedly relocated to one of those right-wing paramilitary communes in Montana or the Pacific Northwest. I have no idea if he's dead or alive, nor do I care."

"Amen," Myles said absently, pointing his flashlight upwards.

"What are you doing?"

"Looking for the bullet hole," he said. "The rifle went off, your dad said, into the ceiling. Hmm…and there it is!" Sure enough, a hole the size of a quarter marred the smooth surface of the plasterboard. "Hold this flashlight," Myles said, pulling a Swiss Army knife from his pants pocket. He handed her the light and began probing inside the hole. More and more chips of paint and plaster fluttered down, and then he quietly said, "Got it." He dug a little deeper and pried out a misshapen silvery-gray slug, which dropped out of the ceiling into the waiting palm of his other hand. "I present you with Exhibit A," he said with satisfaction, and so was quite taken back when his find was met with a flood of tears.

"Marnie, what's the matter?" he said, reflexively pulling her to him.

"What's the *matter?*" she repeated, her words muffled by his shirt. "The fact that it happened anyway, that's what. Yeah, we saved John Lennon that night, but they killed him anyway!"

He held her at arm's length and gently said, "You can't look at it that way. On August 19th, 1966, your dad and you and me helped avoid a disaster that would've marked this city forever. And just look at what we all would've missed if we hadn't prevented it—all the wonderful music and the happiness the Beatles continued to bring people for years to come, with each other and by themselves. Hey, every time I hear a song from *Sgt. Pepper* I smile because I know we made that album possible."

"And the *White Album*, and *Let It Be* and *Abbey Road*."

"Right. So, yeah, maybe things didn't end well for John, but look at how much extra time we bought for him. I'm sure that if he could, he would say thanks."

"I guess you're right," she said, wiping her nose with a tissue. "Hey, would you mind letting me have that bullet? I'd like to bring it to Daddy."

"Sure," he said, pressing it into her palm.

"Want to come along? I'm going over to see him now."

"I'd like that. Let's get out of this place and back into the sunlight. I'll follow you there."

They exited the room, descended the stairs, and were soon outside in the glaring midday sun, walking to their cars whose roofs shimmered in the heat. He followed her out of the parking lot, both of them casting a last look back at the deserted Coliseum.

* * *

The entrance to Elmwood Cemetery, the oldest burial ground in Memphis, was striking, with a crowned stone bridge bordered by stately pillars with a scrolled, wrought iron sign overhead. Marnie slowly navigated her car along the meandering narrow road, beneath ancient elms, oaks and magnolias, until she came to the gravesite area where she pulled over on the grassy shoulder. Myles brought the BMW to a stop right behind her and got out. Together they traversed a section of low profile headstones to the plot where Roy Culpeper lay.

His marker, a four-foot-high by five-foot-wide granite stone, read:

Roy Dean Culpeper
1930—2005
Sgt. US Army, Korean War
Capt. Memphis Police Dept.
Beloved Father and Friend to All

Marnie replanted a small American flag that had fallen over—probably from Memorial Day—and removed the rifle slug from her jacket pocket. "He tried to make a good life for me," she said fondly, laying the slug atop the headstone. "It must've been hard to raise a headstrong girl like me without a wife, but he never complained and Lord knows, he had his own demons from the war to deal with. Now they call it PTSD. Funny thing, though, after that night at the Coliseum, he said the nightmares about Korea stopped."

"Speaking of your mother, did you ever hear from her again?" Myles asked.

"Not a word, ever, and it's just as well. She ran out on us, Myles, and I know she's my mother, but that was unforgivable. Thank God we had Tillie, but she had her own cross to bear."

"You mean, her son?"

"Yeah. Marcus's big dream was to go into the Marines, which he did. He was even decorated for bravery. But then, during our senior year in high school, he went missing near a place called Da Nang. They never found his body.

"For a while, Tillie held out hope, but then it started taking a toll on her and her marriage. Her husband left her, and she eventually went to live with her daughters in Knoxville, where they worked as nurses. She died in the late 70s. I think it was from a broken heart." She blew out a breath and shook her head. "It really bothered Daddy, too. Remember, it was because of his help that Marcus was able to enlist in the first place. As the years went on, my father really soured on the war and what we were doing over there, quite the opposite of the way he felt in the early '60s."

"But overall, your dad had a good life, right?"

"I'd say so. He made it through the King assassination, and even though everyone was expecting there to be rioting here like in many other cities, he helped keep a lid on things and was even commended for how he interacted with the black community. That's why he was promoted to lieutenant when Sutter got the boot and he retired with full honors as a captain.

"Then he did something he always wanted to do— he opened a fishing camp near Pickwick Lake and led a totally stress-free life for the next twenty years. Remember Cecil Blevins, the officer who found us in the room that night? He ended up a sergeant on the force and helped out my father on weekends at the fish camp.

You know, outside of you and me and our parents, he's still the only person who knows what went on that night at the Coliseum, but Daddy swore him to secrecy. Myles, I've never told *anyone* about it, have you?"

"Not a soul."

"Good. It's better kept between us. Anyway, back to Daddy; he never got remarried, though he had a lot of lady friends over the years. I guess my mom turned him off on the commitment thing. But by the time he passed, he was a contented man. He even grew his hair a little longer. Can you imagine?" She smiled at the memory.

"What about you, Marnie?" he asked softly. "Are you happy?"

"Very much so. But I think some apologies are in order."

"Apologies?"

"Listen, Myles," she said, a reassuring hand on his shoulder. "I realize that we kind of went our separate ways in high school. I got into the whole sports thing—I always was a tomboy—and you developed your own relationships. I mean, that kind of stuff happens.

"I don't know if you realize just how much I felt I had to get out of here for a while…all the crummy heat and humidity, the racial tension, the small-minded people all around us…it just wore me out. So, when one of my softball coaches at Central was able to wangle a partial scholarship for me to her alma mater, Colorado U, I grabbed it. I felt bad leaving Daddy alone, but I always came home for my breaks, though I did take summer jobs in Boulder. Then, with a degree in special ed, I got a job teaching and coaching in

Boulder, where I met Bill, who's a physics teacher. Long story short, we've been married thirty years now, with two grown boys who have families of their own. Of course, Daddy came up to visit a few times over the years, and we came down to Memphis, too. Bill and the boys just love Graceland and Beale Street. If we're in town we still go to Charlie Vergos' for ribs and to Dyer's Burgers, just like Daddy and I used to. But I always find myself wanting to get back to Colorado and that crisp mountain air.

"And by the way, I'll have you know that I've brought up my boys—who are of course named John and Paul—the right way. They're Beatles fans from the cradle. Last year for our anniversary they got Bill and me tickets to see Paul McCartney in concert, and it was quite an emotional experience for me. All the memories came flooding back, of Daddy, and you, and 1966. In fact, it was right in the middle of 'Yesterday' that I decided to come back here for our own anniversary."

"I'm glad you did, and that you asked me to join you," he said.

"I had to, Myles." She took a deep breath and wiped away a tear. "I'm sorry I haven't come back for any class reunions. Like I said, I don't see the point in rehashing the nasty stuff of the past. But I need to do a better job of keeping the lines of communication open between us. Maybe I'll even get on Facebook. Then we can see each other all the time. You're allowed to do it, aren't you?"

Myles laughed. "Sure I am. That'll be fun."

"So, tell me," she said, "whatever made you want to end up back here?"

"Barbecued ribs!" he joked. "Seriously, though, as the Beatles would say, it's been a long and winding road.

"Like you, I desperately wanted out of Memphis. So, when I graduated I went back East, to NYU. Meanwhile, my mom got into Alcoholics Anonymous and stopped drinking. When my dad retired, they ended up relocating to Boca Raton, where they still play golf and do whatever 80-somethings do with their time. As for me, I was in my sophomore year in college when, I don't know, I got this 'calling.' I decided right then and there I was switching to religious studies. Ten years later, I was ordained as a rabbi and assigned to a synagogue in Queens. Then, by chance, in 2007, I heard that Temple Israel here in Memphis, my old synagogue, was looking for an associate rabbi, so I packed up the family and came back. It just felt right, and they were happy to have me. Even better, Hannah and the twins hated the winters in New York, so it didn't take too much convincing. We started our family a little later than you, so my girls are still in college, at UT, of course. And yes, they love the Beatles."

"Are you happy?"

He paused. "Yes, very. I was lucky to meet Hannah, the love of my life. But you're the best friend I ever had."

They embraced. "I'm so glad we've found each other again," she said.

"Me, too. Are you going to be heading home?"

"Yes," she said. "This long drive alone has been therapeutic. Besides, school's starting soon. You know that I only have two years to go till retirement? I'm so looking forward to doing a lot of traveling with Bill. Of course, you know England's at the top of the list, first stop Liverpool."

"Surprise, surprise," he joked.

"But, could you do one thing for me today before we say goodbye?"

"Name it."

"Could you do, ah, what's the Jewish prayer for the dead called?"

"Kaddish? You want me to say Kaddish for your father?"

"Yes, Myles. And for Tillie, and her son…and John and George, if that's okay."

"I'd be honored. And, all things considered, I think John and George would approve." He took her hand, bowed his head, and began to pray: "Glorified and sanctified be God's great name throughout the world…"

Author's Note

Although the Memphis concert on the evening of August 19th was not the last of the Beatles' 1966 tour, it was by many accounts the beginning of the end.

From Memphis they flew directly to Cincinnati, Ohio, for an August 20 concert at Crosley Field. However, a torrential rainstorm caused the event to be postponed halfway through, forcing the Beatles to make it up the following day at noon before flying to St. Louis, Missouri for that evening's scheduled concert at the new Busch Stadium, where 23,143 fans sat in the rain as the Beatles, under a makeshift corrugated metal covering that barely held back the storm and threatened them with electrocution, soldiered on through the set.

New York was next, with 11,000 empty seats at Shea Stadium this time, though by all accounts the boys gave a spirited performance. There was also the usual Big Apple craziness, as evidenced when two teenaged girls walked out on the ledge of the 21st floor of the Americana Hotel and threatened to jump unless they met the Beatles. New York City police intervened to avert a possible disaster.

The Beatles then flew cross-country for the final few dates, the first in Seattle, Washington. As had been the case in St. Louis, picketers set up outside the Seattle Coliseum and handed out anti-Beatle leaflets. But again, the fans overwhelmed the naysayers, with a combined 23,000 attending the two shows. They drew 45,000 at Dodger Stadium in Los Angeles but were then blocked by hundreds of fans from leaving the ballpark in their armored vehicle.

By the time the exhausted Beatles took the stage at windswept Candlestick Park in San Francisco on the night of August 29th, 1966, they had secretly reached a unanimous decision that this show would be their last live performance. As a concert experience, this one was rather ordinary, the usual thirty-minute set that ended with "Long Tall Sally," after which John Lennon actually told the crowd, "See you next year."

But he knew better; they all did. On the plane ride afterward, George Harrison announced, "That's it. I'm not a Beatle anymore."

Many Beatle historians point to the Memphis concert, and what has become famous as the "cherry bomb incident" as the final straw that precipitated the decision to never tour again. The grind of travel, isolation in hotel rooms, mind-numbing press conferences, and poor acoustics in concert venues where they could hardly hear themselves, added to the firestorm John Lennon's comments about Christianity had caused, made touring hellish. But also, there was now the actual fear of violence that did not exist in previous years. Whether it was the physical abuse that rained down upon them in Manila or the constant death threats by the KKK and others, the Beatles felt increasingly vulnerable, especially in the US, where John F. Kennedy had been murdered in broad daylight only three years before.

And so, the decision was made to retreat to the only place the foursome were now truly happy—the studio, where they vowed to create the finest rock music ever recorded, employing techniques and electronic wizardry they could never hope to duplicate on stage with three guitars, puny amps and a drum kit. History tells us they made good on this promise with the groundbreaking *Sgt. Pepper's Lonely Hearts Club Band* in 1967. By the time they disbanded in 1970, the Beatles had generated a catalog of music that would be unrivaled and would continue to be enjoyed and loved by generations of fans well into the next millennium.

There are those who would tell you that to see what the Beatles were really about, you had to catch them in those early days at the Cavern Club or the first UK concerts, before the pandemonium their fame generated all but consumed them and reduced their concerts to scripted hit-and-run affairs in which the boys likened themselves to wind-up dolls.

But there are also those devoted fans, like my fictional Marnie Culpeper, who look back years later and proudly say of those wild concerts, "I was *there*. I saw the Beatles!"

Paul Ferrante
February 2018

About the Author

Paul Ferrante is originally from the Bronx and grew up in the town of Pelham, New York. He received his undergraduate and Master's degrees in English from Iona College, where he was also a halfback on the Gaels' undefeated 1977 football team. Paul has been an award-winning secondary school English teacher and coach for over 35 years, as well as a columnist for *Sports Collector's Digest* magazine since 1993 on the subject of baseball ballpark history. Many of his works can be found in the archives of the National Baseball Hall of Fame in Cooperstown, NY. His writings have led to numerous radio and television appearances related to baseball history.

Paul's young adult **T.J. Jackson Mysteries** series has led him to speak at the 150th Anniversary Battle Commemoration in Gettysburg, PA, and the National Baseball Hall of Fame during their 75th Anniversary celebration.

Paul lives in Fairfield, Connecticut and Vero Beach, Florida with his wife Maria and daughter Caroline, a film screenwriter/director.

Please visit Paul's website for information on the **T.J. Jackson Mysteries** and his other writings. Also stop by T.J. Jackson's Facebook page.

www.paulferranteauthor.com
https://www.facebook.com/tjjacksonmysteries/

Also By Paul Ferrante

With Fire & Ice Young Adult Books

The T.J Jackson Mysteries

Last Ghost at Gettysburg
Spirits of the Pirate House
Roberto's Return
Curse of the Fairfield Witch
The Voodoo Cult's Treasure

Adult Novels with Melange Books

The Rovers: A Tale of Fenway

www.ingramcontent.com/pod-product-compliance
Lightning Source LLC
Chambersburg PA
CBHW071558030726
47593CB00001BA/224